THE TEMPLE OF LOVE

The Duke of Inglebury, to avoid the beautiful Lady Charlotte who is determined to marry him, leaves England without saying good-bye having accepted an invitation from the Viceroy of India to help him restore the Taj Mahal and other Temples and Palaces.

When the Duke returns to Government House in Calcutta from investigation of these historic monuments, he finds to his annoyance that Lady Charlotte has just arrived having followed him from England.

The Viceroy has received a letter from the Sultan of Jogyakarta asking for help as the Dutch are neglecting the Buddhist Temples in Java and the thieves are taking away precious treasures from them.

Once again the Duke runs away from Lady Charlotte and leaves at dawn. He arrives in Jogyakarta incognito calling himself Mr. Bury and the Sultan sends him to a special Temple from which a statue of the Buddha has been stolen.

The Duke goes there without anyone being aware of it and finds an exceedingly beautiful girl Sarida, who stares at him in astonishment.

He finds that he has an extraordinary resemblance to the Hindu King who built the Temple in the 9th Century, while Sarida resembles his Consort.

How they are linked together by the Spirits of Java and how they eventually find it impossible to be separated from each other, is told in this unusual and exciting 419th book by BARBARA CARTLAND.

BARBARA CARTLAND

THE TEMPLE OF LOVE

Pan Original
Pan Books London, Sydney and Auckland

First published 1987 by Pan Books Ltd,
Cavaye Place, London SW10 9PG
9 8 7 6 5 4 3 2 1
© Cartland Promotions 1988
ISBN 0 330 30325 2
Printed and bound in Great Britain by
Richard Clay Ltd

ABOUT THE AUTHOR

Barbara Cartland, the world's most famous romantic novelist, who is also an historian, playwright, lecturer, political speaker and television personality, has now written over 450 books and sold over 450 million all over the world.

She has also had many historical works published and has written four autobiographies as well as the biographies of her mother and that of her brother, Ronald Cartland, who was the first Member of Parliament to be killed in the last war. This book has a preface by Sir Winston Churchill and has been republished with an introduction by Sir Arthur Bryant.

"Love at the Helm" a novel written with the help and inspiration of the late Earl Mountbatten of Burma, Great Uncle of His Royal Highness The Prince of Wales, is being sold for the Mountbatten Memorial Trust.

Miss Cartland in 1978 sang an Album of Love Songs with the Royal Philharmonic Orchestra.

In 1976 by writing twenty-one books, she broke the world record and has continued for the following nine years with 24, 20, 23, 24, 25, 22, 26, 25 and 22. In the Guinness Book of Records she is listed as the world's top-selling author.

In private life Barbara Cartland, who is a Dame of Grace of the Order of St. John of Jerusalem, Chairman of the St. John Council in Hertfordshire and Deputy President of the St. John Ambulance Brigade, has fought for better conditions and salaries for Midwives and Nurses.

She has championed the cause for old people, had the law altered regarding gypsies and founded the first Romany Gypsy Camp in the world.

Her designs "Decorating with Love" are being sold all over the U.S.A. and the National Home Fashions League made her in 1981, "Woman of Achievement".

Barbara Cartland's Book "Getting Older, Growing Younger", and her cookery book "The Romance of Food" have been published in Great Britain, the U.S.A., and in other parts of the world.

She has also written a Children's Pop-up Book entitled "Princess to the Rescue".

In 1984 she received at Kennedy Airport, America's Bishop Wright Air Industry Award for her contribution to the development of aviation when in 1931 she and two R.A.F. Officers thought of, and carried, the first aeroplane-towed glider air-mail.

An experiment has taken place with Mrs. Cartland at the moment which has never happened with any author before.

Eagle Moss (Patrick Cavendish) has brought out a hardback book every fortnight at £1.95p. Beautifully bound in red and gold leather it will make a Barbara Cartland Library.

In 1964 she founded the National Association for Health and is now the President, as a front for all the Health Stores and any product made as alternative medicine.

This is now a £300,000,000 turnover a year, with one third going in export.

AUTHOR'S NOTE

Borobudur is the largest Buddhist monument in the world. It was built about the 9th Century, 300 years before Angkor Wat and 200 years before Notre Dame.

Mount Merapi erupted violently about this time covering Borobudur with volcanic ash and concealing her for the greatest part of the millennium.

It was not until 1814 when the English Governor General of Java, Thomas Stamford Raffles, heard rumours of 'a mountain of Buddhist sculptures in stone' and despatched an engineer to investigate.

When the Dutch returned after 4 years of English rule the Temple was forgotten but typical of the attitude of the Dutch officials in 1896 was that 8 cartloads of Borobudur's priceless sculptures were presented to King Chulalongkorn of Siam.

When I visited Indonesia in 1986 I was tremendously impressed with a restoration of Borobudur which is fantastic but I was particularly intrigued by the Temple of Plaosan which was not discovered and restored until 1948.

I found in all the Buddhist Temples a spiritual vibration which was different to anything I felt in other parts of the world but it was particularly vivid in Plaosan which, as I tell in this novel, was built by a Shailendran Princess who was a Buddhist and her husband, King Rakai, the Hindu ruler of Mataram.

Exactly as I have described happening to my hero and heroine, I walked round the beautifully restored gallery and saw a relief of a King who had a strikingly Western face. It was from there that my story began.

Chapter One
1900

Driving from the station towards Government House, the Duke of Inglebury hardly noticed the familiar, over-crowded streets of Calcutta.

There was an endless stream of humanity, a confusion of bullock-carts and the inevitable hawkers of rice-cakes, bananas and betel-nuts.

His thoughts were in fact far away with the magnificent building of the Taj Mahal.

Lord Curzon of Kedleston, the new Viceroy, had arrived in India in 1898.

His great love of architecture had soon made him aware that its architectural heritage had been allowed through the indifference of the Indians, to be almost irretrievably damaged.

He had therefore set himself yet another task in his already abnormally large one.

It was to set in motion a programme of restoration which he himself would personally supervise.

His concern was not limited to Hindu and Islamic monuments, but he was also keenly interested in the British-India buildings of the Georgian period.

It was, the Duke was thinking, as he had thought before, very appropriate that Lord Curzon should find in Government House, Calcutta, a replica of his own ancestral home in Derbyshire.

It was in fact, the Earl of Mornington who in 1798 had decided that the existing Government House, which was in no way superior to the mansions of the leading Calcutta citizens, was unworthy of his station.

He had ordered that it should be pulled down.

The Palace he erected on the site was to become a symbol of the growth of British power.

It had been finished in four years and, although the cost of £63,281 was considered excessive, it was undoubtedly the finest Government House in the world.

The splendour of its Ionic façade was matched only by the admirable simplicity of its great rooms.

The adaptation of a plan of Kedleston Hall in Derbyshire gave it a central block containing the State Apartments, joined to four Wings by curving corridors.

If the Viceroy appreciated it, so did the Duke.

He had not hesitated when he had received an invitation from Lord Curzon asking him to proceed to India immediately.

The Viceroy had explained that he needed his help with the improvements he intended to make at Government House.

Also he wanted his advice on the beautiful and unique Temples of India which were falling into dilapidation because no one had the sense to realise their value.

The Duke was intrigued and he actually had another motive for wishing to leave England at this particular moment.

During the Autumn shooting season he had become involved with Lady Charlotte Denington.

The Duke would have been very stupid if he was not aware that he was undoubtedly the greatest matrimonial 'catch' in Britain at the moment.

He had inherited the Dukedom unexpectedly owing to the death of two more direct heirs.

He had not been pursued so ardently when he was a mere

Subaltern in the Horse Guards.

Although extremely good-looking and well-born, he had not been over-blessed with worldly goods.

He had therefore reached the age of twenty-seven without being pressured up the aisle.

He in fact, enjoyed himself with the sophisticated and very beautiful women with whom the Prince of Wales surrounded himself.

When he had unexpectedly become the 4th Duke of Inglebury, everything had changed.

It was obvious to him that now ambitious mothers spoke to him in a very different tone of voice than they had used previously.

Suitable young women were scattered in front of him like rose-petals in the hope that one of them might become his Duchess.

He had however made up his mind that he had no intention of marrying until everything he possessed was in good order, and until he found somebody he considered worthy to bear his name.

The Burys were an ancient family dating back in history over very many generations.

As far as the Duke could ascertain there had been a few Rakes among them.

But they had certainly never been involved in any scandal nor had they done anything to besmirch or despoil the family name.

Marriage was therefore for the time being out.

Instead he busied himself with making Ingle Castle one of the most comfortable as well as most magnificent private houses in England.

He had no wish to share it with anybody until, as he told himself, he was considerably older.

At the age of thirty-three, he considered himself to be still a young man.

This was not surprising because, as he was so intelligent,

most of his friends were older than himself.

He found that they welcomed him in their company.

George Curzon, who had become Viceroy at the age of thirty-nine, had always had a great affection for the Duke.

He had been determined soon after he arrived in India to have him as one of his guests.

The Duke, as it happened, had so many things to attend to in England that he would not have accepted Lord Curzon's invitation so quickly or with so much pleasure if it had not been for Lady Charlotte.

He had been aware during the Season of the previous year that wherever he went she was invariably present.

Acclaimed by everybody as one of the greatest beauties of the century, she was at the age of twenty-seven at the height of her loveliness.

It would have been impossible for any hostess to give a Ball or a large dinner-party without including her.

She certainly charmed almost every man with whom she came in contact.

The daughter of the Duke of Cambria, she had run away when she was seventeen with Philip Denington.

He was extremely handsome, in fact, devastatingly so, and to a girl of seventeen he must have appeared like a Greek God.

He was however, of little social importance and the Duke of Cambria was furious.

There was nothing he could do about it but accept his son-in-law with a good grace.

He did not pretend however to be upset when Philip Denington riding recklessly in a Steeple-Chase broke his neck.

By this time Charlotte was twenty-four and surprisingly there had been no children of the marriage.

When her year of mourning was over, the Duke and his wife were determined that their daughter should not make a second mistake.

The Duke opened Cambria House in Park Lane.

The first parties they gave there were enough to establish Charlotte as a Beauty who was destined to take London Society by storm.

If her husband had looked like a god, she certainly now looked like a goddess.

She was tall, fair, with a full, almost voluptuous figure, which was the fashion at the moment.

Her skin was the pink-and-white that was proverbially English, and her eyes were the bright blue of forget-me-nots.

Moreover her years with Denington who was a much older man, had taught her how to be witty and amusing.

She would also flirt with any man who approached her in a manner which held him spellbound.

The Duke would have been inhuman if he had not found Lady Charlotte attractive.

He soon learned that the Social World in which they both moved had made up its mind that they were ideally matched to each other.

When he dined at Marlborough House, which he did frequently, Lady Charlotte was always sitting on one side of him.

When he was the guest of one of the great hostesses with whom London abounded, she was there as if it was her right.

He was well aware that they were talked about.

Many of the things that were said to him in his Club as well as in the Ball Rooms had a *double entendre* which insinuated that he was taking a long time in making up his mind.

The Duke could, when he wished, be as cool, aloof and authoritative as Lord Curzon.

The latter was frequently called an "18th century aristocrat born out of his time".

The Duke also certainly resembled one, and had the

grand manner which matched his love of splendid houses and architectural treasures.

He could if he wished be very awe-inspiring.

He would set down any impertinence by raising his eyebrows or with just a look from his steel-grey eyes.

When friends went too far in revealing their curiosity as to how soon he would announce his engagement to Lady Charlotte, they felt as if they had encountered an iceberg.

It was true however that the Duke was asking himself if in fact, he would ever find anybody more suitable to be the Duchess of Inglebury.

Charlotte would grace the Inglebury jewels which were as magnificent as those owned by Princess Alexandra.

When he went to stay with the Marquis of Normington for a pheasant-shoot the last week in October, he was not in the least surprised to find that Lady Charlotte was also a guest.

She was looking, he thought, extremely alluring, even in the sensible tweeds which she wore to accompany the guns.

She sat with him at the first drive.

She made him laugh and flirted with discretion in front of his loader, in a manner he could not help admiring.

She would certainly be an admirable hostess at Inglebury House in Park Lane, and would also, he thought, be equally at home in the country.

Not that he had invited her to Ingle Castle, for the simple reason that it would seem too obvious to those who watched them like hawks.

It was there he would be expected to what was vulgarly called 'pop the question' in the Orangery, or in the enormous Picture Gallery.

This was one of the first rooms in the house he had redecorated.

When he shot with an undeniably skilful right and left a brace of very high pheasants he thought that Lady Charlott's admiring little gasp of surprise was very alluring.

"What am I waiting for?" he asked himself later that evening.

She had come down to dinner wearing a gown of blue chiffon which echoed the colour of her eyes.

He realised that all the other women in the party were jealous of her, just as all the men were envious of him.

Even more so than usual, everybody was making it obvious that it was only a question of time before they were married.

This annoyed him.

He therefore said nothing when the Dowager Marchioness of Normington, who was nearly eighty, slapped his hand playfully with her fan, as he said goodnight to her.

"You are too tardy, young man," she said in a creaking voice. "Remember the fable of the tortoise and the hare, and just be careful that the tortoise does not slip in front of you when you least expect it!"

She laughed at her own joke, displaying her yellowed teeth as she did so.

The Duke felt himself stiffen.

He disliked more than anything else his affairs being talked about in public.

He was aware that several other guests had heard what the Dowager had said and were sniggering.

He had let his valet assist him to undress in silence.

Only when he was alone did he tell himself that he was fed up with people's curiosity and their endless interference with his private life.

He would marry whom he pleased and when he pleased, and he would be damned if he would be pushed into it by old women, or anybody else who had the impertinence to try and meddle.

It was then, to his astonishment, that the door of his bedroom opened and Lady Charlotte came in.

He had not expected her, although it had crossed his mind that, as a widow, it might be expected that she should have a lover.

If however, there had been men in her life, nobody had told him about them.

Because when they met she always seemed to concentrate on him, he had never thought there had been anybody else in a more intimate position.

Now it flashed through his mind that as he had not even kissed her she might have been piqued by his indifference.

Anyway, instead of suggesting that he could come to her, she had come to him, which made it a situation in which he felt nonplussed and not quite certain of what he should do.

There was however no need for him to decide anything.

Lady Charlotte had made up her mind and, as she slipped into bed beside him, there was no question of his deciding whether it was something he wished or did not wish to happen.

Very much later Lady Charlotte murmured against his shoulder.

"I love you, Victor, and I could not imagine any man could be more wonderful or more exciting!"

This was something the Duke had heard from other women, and he was therefore not particularly surprised at Lady Charlotte's reaction to his love-making.

It had certainly been very fiery, in fact incredibly so.

Again the Duke was not surprised.

At the same time, he thought a little cynically that it was invaribly women who looked pink-and-white and very English who became as fierce as tigresses when they were in bed.

"You have made me very happy, Charlotte," he said gently.

She raised her head from his shoulder to look up at him as she said softly:

"That is what I want to do, and you know, Victor, that I love you!"

He did not answer her, finding it easier to kiss her lips which were very near to his than to put anything into words.

Only when she had left him did he realise that he was now very deeply involved in a way that he had tried to avoid.

Lady Charlotte had made it quite clear what she wanted.

Because it was so obvious, every nerve in his body revolted against the pressure of making a decision before he was ready to do so.

He might be slow, he might prevaricate, he might, as the old Dowager had said, be behaving like a tortoise.

But marriage was something which would last a lifetime.

He had no wish to find himself in the position of so many men who were his contemporaries.

No-one could be part of the 'Marlborough House Set' without being aware that the husbands who gathered in White's or Boodles Club early in the evening were complaisently leaving the way free for their wives' lovers to be entertained at home.

The Duke knew that he would expect, although the Social World might call it unreasonable, his wife to be faithful to him.

He could imagine nothing more degrading than being aware that another man had taken his place in his wife's affections.

To know that another man was enjoying the favours that should have been his.

He felt sure from the fact that Charlotte had come to his room and the manner in which her body had melted against his, that it was certainly not the first time she had behaved in such a way.

As a widow he did not condemn her for it, but if she were his wife, it would be a very different matter.

He had known then, firmly and irrevocably, that he would not marry Lady Charlotte, and nothing and nobody could force him into doing so.

Every night while they were staying with the Marquis she had come to him and the last night before the return to London she had asked wistfully:

"When shall we meet again?"

It was quite obvious what she expected his reply to be.

As she kissed his cheek and cuddled a little closer to him the Duke felt as if he was being hypnotised into saying the words she wanted to hear.

It was therefore with a sense of relief that on return to London he had found Lord Curzon's letter waiting for him.

He had made up his mind immediately, telegraphing to the Viceroy his acceptance and leaving, to the astonishment of his household, three days later.

He said no goodbyes and did not inform even his most intimate friends where he was going.

He merely told his secretary to delay answering any enquiries as to his whereabouts for as long as possible.

There must be no question of anybody joining him on the voyage.

This might be possible if they travelled overland to link up with the P. & O. Liner in which he had booked his passage at Marseilles or perhaps Naples.

"I am running away," the Duke told himself with a twist of his lips.

Notes scented with the perfume Lady Charlotte used arrived every day, and there was an invitation from the Duke of Cambria to shoot with him.

There was an invitation too from the Duchess to dine at the end of the week.

The Duke thought with satisfaction that by the time these dates arrived he would be on the high seas.

With his excellent powers of organisation he managed to get away without any difficulty.

Everything was packed and ready, and his valet was looking forward to the voyage as much as he was.

Only when the ship moved down the Suez Canal into the Red Sea did the Duke feel he was really free.

He had the idea the Charlotte would be waiting for him when he returned home, but he would cross that bridge when he came to it.

In the meantime he knew from what George Curzon had said in his letter that he would enjoy India more than he had ever enjoyed it in the past.

He had in fact spent some months there accompanying the Commander-in-Chief of his Regiment as an *Aide-de-camp* when the Marquess of Dufferin was Viceroy.

He had not seen much of the country, but had had to spend what he thought were hours of boredom at *Durbars*, garden-parties, at long-drawn-out dinners and State Balls.

Now he had the suspicion that George Curzon had very different ideas on how he should spend his time, and he was not mistaken.

As soon as he arrived he had been shown the improvements at Government House.

These included electric light, fixed baths instead of the old green painted wooden tubs, electric lifts and electric fans.

The Duke appreciated that the Viceroy had retained the old hand *punkahs* in the marble hall and in the State Apartments, preferring their measured sweep to what he called 'the hideous invention of revolving blades'.

"Absolutely splendid, George!" the Duke had exclaimed. "And just what I might have expected from you!"

"And now come and see what else I have done," the Viceroy said.

He had then produced photographs which had stimulated the Duke's interest and also aroused in him a feeling of excitement.

It somehow had a resemblance to what he felt for a beautiful woman.

The Taj Mahal at Agra, a pearl of inexpressible beauty,

but now marred by neglect and the roughness of the elements, was dirty and dilapidated and in need of urgent repair.

Similarly the Pearl Mosque in the Fort at Lahore Akhari's city of Fatehpur Sikri which had been abandoned when the war in Egypt failed.

There were also the Palace at Mandalay, the ruins of Buapur and dozens of Temples, Mosques and Palaces which had a beauty that was unexampled anywhere else in the world.

They were all being lost to future generations through the stupidity of the Indians and the indifference of the British.

"You will help me?" the Viceroy asked simply.

"Of course," the Duke answered.

He had set out at once for Agra, and what he had found there kept him so entranced that he stayed much longer than Lord Curzon had intended.

But he had speeded the wheels of restoration which Curzon had started, before he reluctantly returned to Calcutta.

He had stopped on the way to look at a Temple that was overgrown with vegetation but beneath it was the most exquisite carving.

He had noted down every detail, taking a number of photographs with one of the latest cameras which he had brought with him from England.

The horses of the carriage turned in at the magnificent gates of Government House and the outriders fell back outside the entrance.

The Duke felt as eager as a young Schoolboy with what he had to relate to his host, knowing how interested Lord Curzon would be.

One of the Viceroy's *Aides-de-camp* was waiting to

welcome him, and when he stepped from the carriage he said:

"Good afternoon, Hancock. Is everything all right?"

"Everything, Your Grace and His Excellency is looking forward to your return. He hopes to be with you as soon as he can get away from a meeting which has already, I expect, proved extremely boring."

The Duke laughed.

"You must give me time to have a bath."

"I suspect," Captain Hancock said, "it was very hot in the train."

"Most unbearably so!" the Duke agreed. "However I was very grateful to be travelling in such comfort."

The Viceregal train newly painted white, had been placed at his disposal.

It had certainly made the journey more comfortable than any he might have been forced to make by ordinary transport.

Trains commanded great respect from the Indians who thought of them as 'magic Monsters'.

But they were invariably over-crowded and inclined, however hard the British tried to prevent it, to arrive late.

The Duke walked towards the North-East Wing where he knew he would be housed.

Despite the magnificence and beauty of Lord Mornington's Palace, the sleeping accommodation was not as adequate as it should have been.

For all its vast size the house was short of bedrooms.

When there were very large parties the guests overflowed into tents on the lawn.

The Duke's rooms, which were those he had occupied before he left, were however very comfortable and as the electric fans were working they were not too hot.

"I hope you will find everything you want, Your Grace,"

Captain Hancock said respectfully.

"I am sure I shall," the Duke answered. 'Who else is staying here?"

Captain Hancock reeled off the names of a number of people, most of whom the Duke thought sounded rather dull.

Then as he drew in his breath to say something, the Captain added:

"A great beauty arrived yesterday with whom I expect Your Grace is well acquainted."

There was a little pause before the Duke asked apprehensively:

"And who is that?"

"Lady Charlotte Denington. She invited herself and of course, as His Excellency knows her father the Duke of Cambria, he was delighted to welcome her."

"Of course!" the Duke said automatically.

Only when the *Aide-de-camp* had left him did he walk frowningly to look out of the window onto the garden.

How could Charlotte dare to follow him so blatantly, he asked himself.

But there was nothing he could do about it, and little he could say.

He was well aware that, like a tigress in the jungle, she was waiting to pounce on him.

"I will not marry her – I will not!" he told himself angrily.

He wondered how he could avoid falling into the trap she had set for him.

He was well aware it would be quickly known in the Social World exactly where she was, and that they were together.

He knew that she was manoeuvring him into a position where, as a Gentleman, he would be forced to repair any damage he might have done to her reputation by offering her a wedding-ring.

She was being extremely clever.

22

The Duke felt like a hunted animal which was aware that it was being surrounded on all sides, and there was no possibility of escape.

"What shall I do?" he asked himself. "What the hell can I do?"

He wondered if he should say to the Viceroy that it was imperative he should return immediately to his supervision of the restoration work at the Taj Mahal.

Alternatively, he could set off for a tour of India to inspect all the other buildings of which Lord Curzon had shown him photographs.

But he was certain that if he suggested this Lady Charlotte would insist eagerly on going with him.

If she appealed to the Viceroy or worse still, to his gentle wife Mary, who always thought the best of everybody, it would be impossible for him to refuse to take her.

The Duke had a bath and changed his clothes.

He was nearly ready when one of the servants, dressed in the scarlet and gold uniform of the Viceroy's staff, came to tell him that Lord Curzon was waiting for him.

The Duke picked up his notes.

He then walked the lamentably long distance between the bedrooms and the Viceroy's Private Sitting-Room which was in the South-West Wing.

It was a relief when he entered the room to find that Lord Curzon was alone and sitting at a desk with a pile of papers in front of him.

He rose to his feet, with an expression of pleasure, making him look far younger than he was, on his face.

"You are back, Victor!" he exclaimed. "It is delightful to see you!"

"I have a lot to tell you," the Duke said.

"I am waiting to hear it," Lord Curzon replied, "and I also have something to tell you which I know will surprise you."

The Duke was too eager to show his photographs and to

read out his notes to pay much attention to what Lord Curzon had just said.

It was an hour later when he had explained exactly what he had seen that the Viceroy said, leaning back in his chair:

"You have helped me enormously, Victor, and I cannot be grateful enough to you for helping me in this way. Heaven knows, there is a great deal more to be done."

"At least you have made a beginning," the Duke said, "but I agree with you, it will take a lifetime, or several lifetimes, to save what needs to be saved throughout the whole country."

As he spoke he thought that this was the moment when he should suggest to Lord Curzon that he set off at once on another exploration, and alone.

Before he could speak however, Lord Curzon said:

"I have here a letter which will surprise you as it surprised me, and I feel that something should be done about it. I am sure moreover you are the only person who can help me."

The Duke was listening, wondering what the Viceroy could possibly have to say to him.

He found it impossible not to keep thinking of Charlotte waiting for his appearance. She would, he thought, be determined to proclaim to the Curzons exactly what their relationship was.

She would do it so cleverly and with such subtlety that they would not even suspect that it was an act.

At the same time she would make it very clear that she was to be the Duchess of Inglebury.

"What can I do?" the Duke's mind was crying out.

Almost childishly he wished he had a magic carpet on which he could fly away from Government House into another part of the world where she could not reach him.

The Viceroy found the letter he was seeking and unfolding it said as he did so:

24

"I have had this translated into English because I thought it was easier for us both to understand. But I believe in fact you speak Javanese."

"Javanese?" the Duke asked incredulously.

The Viceroy nodded.

"This is from the Sultan of Jogyakarta. He has written to me confidentially because, as he says in very flowery language, he has learned of my intention to restore the treasures of India and begs me on his knees to assist him."

"In what way?" the Duke asked.

"You have heard of course," the Viceroy said, "of the magnificent Temple of Borobudur."

The Duke thought for a moment, then he said:

"It is in central Java, and unless I am mistaken, Stamford Raffles, when he was Lieutenant-Governor of Java in a brief period of British rule during the Napoleonic wars, discovered Borobudur."

"Exactly," the Viceroy said, "I knew you, of all people, would remember that Raffles in 1814 ordered it to be cleared."

"What happened?" the Duke asked.

"The work was supposed to be continued when the Dutch came back into power," the Viceroy replied.

He paused for a moment and the Duke said:

"And the Sultan has written to you about that? I do not suppose there is much you can do about it, and the Dutch will hardly welcome your interference."

"The Sultan is well aware of that," Lord Curzon replied, "but he tells me that he has knowledge of another Temple of great importance which is nearer to Jogyakarta. According to him it has not yet been discovered, nor are the Dutch aware of it."

The Duke raised his eyebrows but he did not speak as the Viceroy went on:

"The Sultan says the Temple is unique, which is why he

asks, in fact begs, that I shall come myself, which of course is impossible. Alternatively that I should send somebody to prevent it from being desecrated."

"In what way?" the Duke enquired.

"Apparently by thieves if the site is opened up and explored."

The Duke sighed.

It was a story he had heard only too often in Greece and Egypt, and in any other part of the world where there were objects of historic interest which could be sold to collectors.

"I want you to read the Sultan's letter," the Viceroy said, "and I cannot help feeling, Victor, it would be worth your while to visit Jogyakarta."

The Duke stared at him in astonishment before he asked:

"Are you serious?"

"Very serious," Lord Curzon replied, "and knowing of the magnificence of Borobudur, which apparently is only appreciated by the English, I feel it impossible for me to ignore this plea from the Sultan."

He paused before he added:

"Perhaps – one never knows – here is another 'Borobudur' which must be saved for posterity, not only from neglect, but also from the Dutch who have no respect for Eastern religions or for that matter the treasures of Java."

Lord Curzon spoke violently because he minded so fervently if relics of historic interest were neglected or destroyed.

It was then, as the Duke listened to him, he realised that here, when he had least expected it, was his own salvation.

Chapter Two

The Duke felt elated, thinking with relief that the Viceroy had solved his pressing problem.

Then he was aware that Lord Curzon was still looking at the letter from the Sultan.

There was an expression on his face which told the Duke all too clearly how angry he was.

"After I received this letter," he said, "I made some enquiries, of course as secretly as possible." The Duke looked puzzled, but he did not interrupt and the Viceroy went on:

"I learnt to my horror that four years ago, in 1896, the Dutch officials made a presentation of eight cart-loads of unique relics of Borobudur as souvenirs to King Chula-longkorn of Siam who was visiting them."

"I do not believe it!" the Duke exclaimed.

"Unfortunately it is true," Lord Curzon said, "and the gift included thirty relief panels, five Buddha statues, two lions, and a guardian sculpture."

"It seems incredible that they should do such a thing!" the Duke exclaimed.

"Many of these now irreplaceable works of art have already ended up in private collections," Lord Curzon said bitterly.

There was a pause before he added:

"Besides which, as you will understand Victor, the thieves moved in and thousands of other small but priceless

27

pieces of art were removed surreptitiously."

"I cannot believe that the Dutch would be so irresponsible as to destroy the treasures of Java!" the Duke said.

Even as he spoke he knew that the Dutch were not a particularly artistic people when it concerned anything Eastern.

He had also heard vaguely stories of the way in which the Temples of Bali had been treated.

Lord Curzon bent forward on his desk.

"You will understand now, Victor, why I am telling you that any help I can give the Sultan must be done secretly, and without the Dutch being aware that I am interested."

"I should have thought that might prove an impossibility," the Duke said.

"I thought that myself until, reading further the very fulsome letter from the Sultan, I found that the Dutch so far have no knowledge of the Temple about which he is speaking, and he has apparently confided only in one most trusted adviser."

The Duke sat back in his chair.

"What do you suggest I do?"

Lord Curzon smiled.

"The answer to that is to get there as quickly as you can and, if nothing else, prevent the thieves from desecrating it."

'Do you think the Temple has already been rifled?" the Duke asked.

"The Sultan writes as if he suspects that is intended."

The Duke thought for a moment. Then he said:

"When I left England in response to your invitation, my yacht was at the ship-builders having a few repairs done. I told my secretary to see that it followed me here as quickly as possible."

Lord Curzon smiled as he said:

"I have ascertained that it is already in the harbour!"

The Duke laughed.

"Really, George," he exclaimed, "you are fantastic! Does anything, however small, escape your eagle eye?"

"Not if I can help it!" the Viceroy answered.

"Then I imagine if I have to land at Java without anybody being aware of it," the Duke went on, "I should go there in my own yacht, but of course, not using my title."

'I have already thought of that," the Viceroy replied, "and 'Bury' is quite an ordinary name, at least in Java!"

The Duke laughed again.

"My family would be insulted, but I am quite content to admit to Bury, so long as you make sure that the Sultan realises he can trust me in the same way that he trusts you."

"There will be no doubt about that," the Viceroy said. "The Sultan's letter was brought here by one of his personal *Aides-de-camp* and the man has been waiting on my instructions for your return."

The Duke's eyes twinkled.

He did not say anything, but he knew that his friend was enjoying explaining to him his complicated plan in detail.

"Now you have agreed to do what I ask," Lord Curzon continued, "the Javanese will leave tonight with a letter for the Sultan, who will be told to expect 'Mr. Bury', as soon as you can get there. He must make quite sure that the Dutch have no idea that an Englishman is to be his guest."

'I am only grateful," the Duke said a little sarcastically, "that you do not expect me to disguise myself in a *sarong* or if we are to speak Javanese, a *kain*!"

"I think," Lord Curzon replied, "you will give the girls a treat by looking as you are."

"Girls?" the Duke exclaimed. "As I shall not be allowed to meet any of the Sultan's Concubines, the only women I am likely to see will be carved in stone!"

The Viceroy thought this amusing.

Then after he had teased the Duke he asked in a more serious tone:

"When will you leave?"

"Tomorrow," the Duke replied, "and on my own terms."

The Viceroy raised his eyebrows before he asked:

"And what are those?"

"Quite simply – that no one, not even your wife, knows where I am going. When I vanish from Government House you merely say casually that you have had an urgent message from those repairing the Taj Mahal and on your instructions I hurried back to find out what was wrong."

There was a little pause as the Duke finished speaking.

Then Lord Curzon asked:

"Any particular reason for this 'cloak and dagger', secrecy?"

"Every reason!" the Duke replied.

He got up as he spoke and walked to the window to look out onto the garden.

The sun was a ball of fire through the trees, and there were a large number of gardeners watering the grass to keep it green.

They were also many others tending the flowers.

The garden, the Duke remembered, was not limited to flowers or the insect kingdom.

Several Governor-General's wives, including Lady Canning, had complained of the monkeys.

One had invaded Lady Canning's dressing-room, breaking her china and carrying off her French servant's parrot. But she had been particularly troubled by bats.

"One evening," she wrote, "I had five bats in my bedroom flying about and squeaking!"

Although the Duke had been at Government House only a few days after arriving in India, he had already heard that the jackals were being tiresome.

At night they would emerge from the drains to howl in the shrubberies.

One of the *Aides-de-camp* told him that what he really

disliked were the stinking civet cats which would clamber up the pillars and drain-pipes on the roof of the house.

Sometimes they even entered the bedrooms on the South side.

Mary Curzon told him she awoke once to find one five feet long, drinking the glass of milk by her bedside.

The Duke had thought this must be an exaggeration, but he was prepared to believe that Lord Curzon with his usual eye for detail, had eliminated most of them.

The same applied to the flying foxes who flung themselves from tree to tree.

This all passed through his mind simply because he was thinking that Lady Charlotte was as dangerous as a wild animal.

Whether she went up a drainpipe or came down from the roof, she would somehow come into his bedroom tonight.

He was silent for so long that finally Lord Curzon asked:

"What is the matter, Victor? I know you are worried about something and it is unlike you to be so reticent about it."

The Duke's impulse was to answer that if there was one thing he disliked it was talking about his love-affairs.

But he felt sure that the moment Lord Curzon and his wife saw him and Lady Charlotte together she would contrive to make them believe that they were desperately in love.

'There is one among your guests," he said finally, "who has followed me to India. Quite frankly, George, I ran away to be rid of her, but she is exceedingly persistent, and the only way I can be free of her is to disappear."

He knew without saying any more that Lord Curzon would guess to whom he was referring, and with his able and quick mind would understand exactly what the Duke intended.

There was only a slight pause before Lord Curzon said: ·

"In which case, it would be best if you left at dawn."

'That is what I would like to do," the Duke replied.

"Very well," Lord Curzon agreed. "Everything will be arranged and one of my *Aides-de-Camp* will have a carriage waiting for you to carry you to the harbour. No-one – I repeat *no-one* – shall have any idea where you have gone."

The Duke sighed with relief.

"Thank you, George," he said, "I am very grateful."

"Everything you need to take with you will be ready," Lord Curzon said sharply almost as if he was giving himself orders, "and there will be maps for the Captain of your yacht showing the coastline nearest to Jogyakarta."

He paused before he went on:

'It should not be difficult for you to find some sort of transport, although not perhaps a very comfortable one, by which you can reach the Sultan, but I have already ascertained that Jogyakarta is not much more than thirty miles from the sea."

"Thank you," the Duke said again.

The Viceroy then pressed a bell on his desk and a moment later the door opened and an *Aide-de-Camp* stood there.

"They are waiting for Your Excellency in the Throne Room!" he announced.

Without saying any more to his friend, the Viceroy left his Sitting-Room.

The Duke, sitting down in a comfortable chair, picked up the newspapers which had arrived that morning from England.

He made no effort to get in touch with the rest of the house-party, and when he was dressed for dinner, he deliberately came downstairs with only a few minutes to spare.

At last he reached the Drawing-Room and thought the two *Aides-de-Camp* on duty looked at him reproachfully as if they had been nervous of his being too late.

There was only just time to greet some of the guests who had congregated in the vast but comfortable Drawing-Room which was used for such occasions.

It was impossible that anything should not run smoothly, when George Curzon had a greater appreciation of the customs and traditions of Government House than any other Viceroy who had preceded him.

In fact, he had brought the running of the Viceregal Court to perfection.

As the Duke moved through a great number of rooms and down several staircases, he could see how Lord Curzon had restored and modernised the building, improving the furnishings and filling in gaps in the collection of portraits.

Looking extremely impressive in his evening-clothes and wearing his decorations, the Duke greeted those guests he had met before and an *Aide-de-Camp* introduced him to some newcomers.

He was aware long before he reached Lady Charlotte that she was looking at him with shining eyes.

She was undeniably exceedingly beautiful as she stood glittering with jewels that eclipsed any of those worn by the other ladies.

Her tiara of turquoises and diamonds was a complement to her blue eyes, and a necklace of the same stones made her white skin seem dazzling.

Her gown was as elaborate as if she was being presented at Buckingham Palace, and she carried in her hand a painted fan with a handle of mother-of-pearl.

"I believe you know Lady Charlotte Denington, Your Grace," the *Aide-de-Camp* was saying.

But as Lady Charlotte reached out her hand towards him the Duke turned away.

There was a signal from another *Aide-de-Camp* and the guests quickly moved to their appropriate places, standing stiffly almost at attention.

The door opened and the Viceroy and Vicereine came in.

They were flanked on either side by *Aides-de-Camp* and as they proceeded to greet their guests the ladies curtsied and the Gentlemen bowed their heads as to Royalty.

Not a word was spoken except by the Viceroy and his wife and the person whom they were greeting.

Only when the formalities were completed was there a general relaxation and the slight murmur of lowered voices.

There was no time for the Duke to speak to Lady Charlotte, even though he was aware that she was moving towards him.

The procession was forming behind the Viceroy who led the way to the Dining-Room.

The Duke found himself escorting the very attractive wife of the French Ambassador.

As he knew Paris well and had met a number of her relatives and friends, they had a great deal to talk about.

But it was impossible for him not to realise that Lady Charlotte's eyes on the other side of the table were continually on him.

It made it hard for him to concentrate on what Lady Curzon who was on his other side, was saying.

People who found the Viceroy difficult and too pompous adored Mary Curzon.

An American, it was not until she reached Bombay in December 1898 that she realised the extraordinary distinction and isolation of the position which she and her husband were to occupy.

She wrote home:

"We might as well be Monarchs."

They had gone ashore from the Liner which had conveyed them to a landing-stage which was covered in crimson cloth, and after speeches of welcome drove the

34

seven miles to Government House through packed streets lined with soldiers.

Above their heads was held a golden umbrella, one of India's most ancient and venerable symbols of Royalty.

Mary accepted with pleasure the endless grandeur by which she was surrounded from that moment.

She seemed not to mind being stared at and was never at a loss for the right word or gesture.

She also knew instinctively when to allow her husband to take precedence and when to advance ahead of him.

That the two most important people in the land were very much in love with each other did not pass unnoticed by the Indians, who worshipped Krishna the God of Love.

Of course, Mary found the house extraordinary and, as she wrote home, 'very inconvenient'.

Dressing in the evening by the light of smoking candles was difficult, and she found it impossible to make her friends in England understand that the kitchen was not even in the house.

It lay 200 yards away in a Calcutta back street, and every dish had to be carried across the gardens in wooden boxes.

On their arrival the gardens had housed a menagerie of terrifying animals.

Flying foxes flung themselves from tree to tree until Curzon had them shot.

But to be with the man she loved Mary Curzon was prepared to put up with anything, even her own ill-health which grew progressively worse owing to the Indian climate.

She talked to the Duke in her soft, sweet voice and at the same time kept looking towards her husband as if to re-assure herself he was there.

As she did so the Duke thought that she was exactly the sort of wife he wanted for himself.

He could not imagine her for one moment being unfaithful or even wanting to flirt with another man.

She had waited such a long time to marry George Curzon and now, as if she told the Duke, "to be together is like being in Heaven".

'The trouble is,' the Duke thought when dinner was ended, 'there are too few "Mary Curzons" in the world, and far too many "Lady Charlotte Deningtons"!'

He did not miss the fact that, perhaps hoping to make him jealous, Lady Charlotte had been making herself conspicuous with the attractive-looking man who had taken her down to dinner.

She appeared to laugh a little more loudly than the other guests, and several times during the meal he had raised his glass to her.

By the expression in his eyes the Duke knew he was toasting her with words of love.

The Duke visualised this sort of behaviour taking place at Ingle Castle.

If it did, he would want to beat his wife, and certainly to insult the man concerned, even to the point of challenging him to a duel.

All of which would cause a highly undesirable and obnoxious scandal which must be avoided at whatever the cost to himself.

He could not help realising that his visit to Java would doubtless be very uncomfortable since he would have to travel incognito.

He might find himself having to endure a great many inconveniences which would not have occurred had he been able to use his title.

Anything however would be better than staying and facing, as he was sure he would have to do, what Lady Charlotte was intending.

When finally the gentlemen joined the ladies, there followed, as was usual in India, the immediate departure of the guests who were not staying in the house.

The Duke had always thought it was a most pleasant aspect of Indian hospitality that they did not have to linger on yawning the hours away.

There was no need to make desultory conversation or to listen, as one did in England, to some loud-voiced female singing an aria from some Opera, which he had never thought suitable in a Drawing-Room.

Instead the guests left at a pleasantly early hour, and as soon as they had done so the Viceroy and his wife also said goodnight.

As Lord Curzon shook the Duke by the hand he said:

"Follow me, I have a last instruction to give you."

The Duke was delighted.

He was well aware that Lady Charlotte was moving through the guests towards him and in a few seconds it would have been impossible to avoid her any longer.

He therefore followed the Curzons from the room, and when they were outside the Viceroy said:

"I have something to give you."

He then turned to his wife to say:

"I will follow you, darling. There is a letter just arrived which I want Victor to see."

Mary Curzon smiled.

"Please do not be too long, George," she said. "We were so late last night, and you have done so much today that I am sure you must be tired."

As she spoke she looked pleadingly at the Duke, who said quietly:

"I promise I will not keep him long."

Lady Curzon smiled at both men and went on up the stairs.

'The Duke and Lord Curzon walked towards the Sitting-Room.

"I suddenly remembered when I was dressing," Lord

Curzon said, "that you would not have any Javanese money, and it might cause comment if you were trying to use either English pounds or Indian *rupees*."

"I have known you for years, George," the Duke remarked, "but you continue to amaze me! If there was a 'Minister of Efficiency' in Parliament, the place would be yours by right!"

'Most people complain that I am too efficient," Lord Curzon remarked.

He spoke a little bitterly, and the Duke was aware that his efforts to achieve perfection had inevitably made him a number of enemies.

On the desk in his private room there was a packet of money which he handed to the Duke.

"This should last you until you are with the Sultan in Jogyakarta," Lord Curzon said. "Then, I am quite certain, he will be able to supply you with money and anything else you may require."

"I hope so," the Duke answered, "and thank you. For, if I am helping you, you are also helping me."

Lord Curzon looked at him.

"She is very beautiful, Victor! Are you quite certain you are not making a mistake?"

"Quite certain!" the Duke said firmly.

The two men walked back the way they had come and parted at the top of the stairs.

The Duke went to his bedroom in the North-East Wing where he found his valet waiting for him.

He had already told Dawson, who had been with him for some years, that they were leaving at dawn tomorrow.

He knew he could trust him not to tell any of the other servants.

As he entered the room he saw that everything that had been unpacked before he changed for dinner had now been replaced in the trunks.

Dawson was only waiting for the clothes he was still wearing.

As the Duke took off his decorations he said to Dawson:

"I hope we do not make any noise in the morning. Who are our neighbours?"

Dawson – who always had a knowledge of everything – reeled off six names and the seventh was the one for which the Duke was waiting.

"Lady Charlotte Denington's in the room on the corner," Dawson said. "I understands 'Er Ladyship arrived from England yesterday in a ship wot 'ad a bad passage through the Bay of Biscay."

"Tomorrow we must find out how the *Sea-Hawk* fared," the Duke remarked casually.

"Is that 'ow we're travellin', Your Grace?"

"It is!" the Duke answered.

"Well, that suits me," Dawson replied. "I always feels more at 'ome with those as speaks English, than with them twisty-tongued languages, if Your Grace knows what I mean."

"I know exactly," the Duke replied, "but I am afraid it will not be for long."

Dawson picked up his shoes and shrugged his shoulders.

"Oh, well," he said, "if it ain't one thing in life, it's another, and there's nothin' to be done about it!"

"Nothing!" the Duke agreed.

At the same time, he told himself he was being a fool.

He was quite certain that as soon as he was alone Lady Charlotte could come to his room as she had in England.

He thought that, if he allowed her to stay, it would only accentuate her determination to make him marry her.

It was then, suddenly, as Dawson was preparing to leave, that he had an idea.

All the time he had been working on the Taj Mahal, because it had been so hot, he had slept on the roof, as most

Indians did.

But it was something it had never crossed his mind he might do at Government House.

Now he said to Dawson:

"I would much rather sleep out of doors than here with these fans turning all night. I am sure they will keep me awake."

"As it 'appens, Your Grace," Dawson said, "I've already found out there's a flat roof just above us, which be used occasionally by one of 'Is Excellency's *Aides-de-Camp*."

"Then that is where I shall sleep," the Duke said, "and we will go there straight away."

He was worried as he left his room in case he should encounter Lady Charlotte on the way, but to his relief all the doors along the passage were closed.

Dawson led him to where halfway along the corridor there was a small subsidiary staircase which took them up onto the roof.

The stars were brilliant overhead and the Duke could see through the trees the lights of the town.

It seemed very quiet, and there was certainly no sound of jackels or of flying foxes, since Lord Curzon had them destroyed.

There were three mattresses on the roof, and Dawson had carried with him up the stairs a pillow and a light blanket.

The Duke lay down on a mattress which he found quite comfortable.

Dawson put the blanket down beside him knowing it was unlikely he would want it, but it would be there if he did.

"I'll call Your Grace at 'alf-past four," Dawson said.

"Make it punctual," the Duke replied, "and thank you Dawson!"

"Goodnight, Your Grace."

The valet walked away and the Duke thought with a faint smile that he could sleep without fear of being disturbed by Lady Charlotte.

He thought it would amuse the *Aides-de-Camp* in the morning when they learned where he had spent the night.

It would doubtless be repeated to Lord Curzon when he asked if he had got off without any difficulty.

If Lady Charlotte tried to make trouble about their relationship, she would find it hard to substantiate it.

"I have been very clever!" the Duke congratulated himself, "and in future I will take care to keep away from all women who may want to marry me."

He thought as he spoke that if he wanted female companionship or something more intimate, there were always the married Beauties who delighted the Prince of Wales.

Like the fascinating French Ambassadress he had sat next to at dinner, they were prepared to look provocatively at any man they met.

"I shall remain a bachelor for the next twenty years at least!" the Duke decided.

He shut his eyes because the stars were so vivid that he thought they would keep him awake.

The Duke was fast asleep when he heard Dawson say in a low voice:

"It's just after half-past four, Your Grace!"

The Duke was instantly alert.

He was used to rising early, and now while escaping from Lady Charlotte he was starting off on a new and exciting adventure!

It was different from anything he had done before.

He had travelled a great deal, but since inheriting the title he had become of such importance that he was escorted by Couriers, Station-Masters or *Aides-de-Camp* wherever he went.

When he went to Ingle Castle he travelled in his own private train, and the same applied when he journeyed to Scotland.

Coming out to India, even though it was at a moment's notice, it was not difficult for his secretary to have him provided with one of the best cabins on the P. & O. Liner.

There was also an adjacent one which was turned into a Sitting-Room for him.

His valet was opposite him on the same deck.

The Duke in fact, had grown used, as had Lord Curzon, to being of such importance that he was treated like Royalty.

Now he had to prepare himself to be not only in a strange country he had never visited before, but also to be to his host the Sultan, nothing more than a substitute for Lord Curzon.

He was quite certain he would be treated hospitably and politely, but that was not the same as being the Duke of Inglebury.

All the same, even if he had to disguise himself as a street-sweeper or a rickshaw-wallah, it would be better than finding himself inescapably tied by a golden ring to Lady Charlotte.

When he returned to England there was of course, always the chance that she would be waiting for him.

But he was prepared to believe that by that time she would have become engaged to somebody else.

He was well aware there were few men who could offer her what he could but at the same time, Charlotte could not afford to wait for ever.

The Duke prayed in his heart that she would be impatient, when she found he had gone, and would accept defeat and look elsewhere.

When he left Government House by a side entrance and was escorted through the streets by a tired *Aide-de-Camp*, he could not help feeling it was the beginning of a drama.

The curtain was rising, but he was not certain what the Play would be about.

The Viceroy's carriage carried him swiftly through the almost empty streets.

He could see on the pavements the dark bundles which were Indians still sleeping, as he had slept, on the roof.

There were a few pariah dogs scratching about in the refuse looking for something to eat.

There was the occasional woman, her face covered, searching as the dogs were for scraps of food that the hotels had thrown away.

It was so early that even the sacred cows were still lying down.

The stars were beginning to fade, and the Duke knew that in a few minutes there would be the first glimmer of dawn.

Then all India would spring to life.

They reached the harbour, and he saw with pleasure the elegant lines of the *Sea Hawk* where she lay at the quayside, the lights shining from her portholes.

There were Seamen on duty at the foot of the gangplank, and he was aware the Captain was on deck waiting for him to step aboard.

He had already told the *Aide-de-Camp* how excellently he had slept in the open air.

Now as the young man assisted him from the carriage he shook him by the hand and said:

"Goodbye, Captain Hancock, and thank you for looking after me."

"It has been a pleasure, Your Grace," the *Aide-de-Camp* replied, "and on His Excellency's order no-one shall know where you have gone. Your secret, I assure you, is safe in my keeping."

"I am quite certain of that," the Duke smiled.

He walked up the gang-plank, aware as he did so that another carriage which was carrying Dawson and the luggage had drawn up behind his own.

The Seamen saluted him and as he stepped on deck the Captain said:

"Good morning, Your Grace, it is a great pleasure to have you with us again!"

"I hear you had a bad passage in the Bay," the Duke commented.

"Not so bad that we had any breakages or trouble with the yacht, Your Grace, and I think you would have been proud of the way she stood up to the elements."

"I am sure I should!" the Duke replied. "Put to sea, Captain, and I will join you on the bridge."

The Captain saluted and the Duke, having walked into the Saloon, put down the papers he had been carrying with the exception of the map of Java.

It was a large and very comprehensive one, as was to be expected coming from the Viceroy.

As soon as they had moved out of harbour the Duke went on the bridge and showed the Captain where they were heading.

He knew that the Officer was intrigued.

"I was not expecting we'd be going to Java, Your Grace, and if we did . . it would be to Jakarta where there's an excellent port from which they ship a great deal of wood and other commodities aboard."

"I am aware of that," the Duke said, "but I want you to understand, Captain Barrett, that this is a very private visit and I have no wish for the Dutch to know who I am. I shall therefore be known simply as 'Mr. Bury'."

The Captain looked surprised, then he said:

"The Dutch'll certainly be disappointed to miss Your Grace. From what I know of them, they're very fond of titles, especially the Governor General Van der Wyik."

44

"I have heard of him," the Duke said, "but I have no wish to come into contact with any of them at this moment. In fact, make it clear to the crew, Captain, that no-one – I repeat no-one – is to let the Dutch, or anyone else, know my real identity."

"I'll make sure your orders are obeyed, Your Grace," the Captain replied.

The Duke stayed on deck until the sun was shining, and he was aware that they were heading at a good speed down the Indian Ocean.

It was then once again that he was thinking this was not only an adventure, but something new that had never happened to him before.

It was certainly a change from the parties, the Balls, the gossip, and *affaires de coeur* of Mayfair.

It was also a change from the quiet serenity of Ingle Castle, the problems of running the estate, and the inevitable decisions as to whom he should invite to stay to prevent himself from being bored.

'This is new – quite new!' he thought.

With the sun glittering on the sea he suddenly felt curiously elated.

He had the feeling that on this journey he would find something he had never found before.

Not only something as precious as the Taj Mahal, but something specially for himself!

It could be something personal, something different from anything he had experienced so far in his life, either physically or spiritually.

Then he knew he was just romanticising, and he mocked at himself for letting his imagination run away with him.

As he went to the Saloon for breakfast, he was smiling, but a little cynically.

Chapter Three

After breakfast the Duke inspected the papers Lord Curzon had given him.

Some he had received the previous night, but some had been handed to him only that morning by an *Aide-de-Camp*.

Amongst them was a personal note, and when he opened it he was aware that George Curzon must have written to him in the middle of the night.

It was so like him, the Duke thought, to be thinking over the details of a plan even when he was in bed with somebody as beautiful and alluring as his wife.

He had written:

> *"I suggest you tell anyone who is interested that you are a tourist writing an article for the National Geographic Magazine. Even the Dutch will accept that with a certain amount of respect and it will explain why you have a camera with you.*
>
> *Bon voyage, and good luck.*
>
> *George."*

Thinking it over, the Duke decided it was a good idea.

With his camera, which was the latest to appear in London, he had already taken some excellent photographs of the Taj Mahal.

He hoped he could take some in Indonesia which George would enjoy seeing, and perhaps later he would be able to visit the islands himself.

The Duke had always intended to go to Java.

After he had been India the first time, because he was interested in all Oriental languages, he had learnt a little Javanese, enough to make himself understood.

Also, provided they spoke slowly he could understand the Javanese in what they were trying to say.

He thought it was unlikely that he would find many people there who spoke English, and he was quite certain the Javanese would not speak Dutch if they could help it.

Their hatred for their rulers was understandable, especially when, as the Duke knew, the Dutch had been very harsh with them.

Wars upon the tribes had killed, it was calculated, thousands upon thousands.

At the back of his memory the Duke recalled the war in Central Java which had been an unusually bloody conflict and had lasted for five years.

It had cost the Dutch some 15,000 soldiers. Javanese losses, however, were somewhere in the vicinity of 200,000.

Both sides had lost a substantial number from disease, and for the Javanese there was also the scourge of famine.

"They certainly suffered," the Duke murmured.

He thought he had a great sympathy for a people who had fought so valiantly for their freedom.

He could understand how much it infuriated Lord Curzon to think now of their treasures being either given away or stolen.

He knew that the work the Viceroy was doing in India was something for which, when he died, he would always be remembered.

It was very hot in the afternoon when the Duke sat reading the notes with which George Curzon had provided him.

He was planning what he should do as soon as he stepped ashore.

It should not be difficult for him to reach Jogyakarta.

At the same time, he could not help wishing that he was a little more certain exactly how he could get there.

Two days later, just after dawn, the '*Sea Hawk*' steamed into one of the small bays which Lord Curzon had encircled with red ink on the map.

The Captain had chosen the first one and found the water was deep enough for the yacht to move quite close to the shore.

On the map at any rate, it was the shortest distance from Jogyakarta.

The Duke, with Dawson, was rowed ashore, taking with them the minimal amount of luggage that would be necessary for perhaps a three week stay.

The Duke hoped that by that time he would have found out everything that Lord Curzon wanted to know.

Alternatively if there was anything he should inspect in other parts of the island, he could return first to the yacht.

He had given the Captain instructions to move some way out to sea so as not to be noticed, but to keep a continual watch on the land.

He would signal to the *Sea Hawk* when he wished to be collected.

On his instructions, Dawson had discarded his habitual uniform.

It would have made him conspicuous and instantly recognisable as a European gentleman's valet.

Dawson therefore wore almost the same type of clothes as his master, a light tropical suit and a shirt which had little to distinguish it from the shirts worn by any ordinary man in the East.

On their heads they wore broad-brimmed hats rather than the conventional *topee* which they left in the yacht.

They stepped ashore and climbed a twisting stony path up the low cliffs.

The last stars were still shining in the sky, and although

there was a faint light from the East, dawn had not yet broken.

The land around them was almost in darkness.

As the Duke walked off briskly followed by Dawson carrying his cases, he saw that only a very short distance inshore were the inevitable padi-fields.

The Duke was aware that in Java after the end of the war in 1830 the Dutch had introduced the Culture System.

It required each peasant to grow certain commercial crops for the Government, generally using two-fifths or more of his land for the enforced cultivation of these products.

Production had shot up to new heights, but the farmers were resentful and the peasants loathed their forced labour.

They prayed for a Prince who would come and rescue them from their current misery.

It meant however that a great deal more of the land was cultivated than had ever been before.

As dawn broke the Duke could see the natives in their huge hats coming to work in the paddy-fields.

A resigned obedience concealed the rebellious feelings in their hearts.

The Duke aroused little attention as he and Dawson walked on until they came to a rough road.

Then he saw to his relief that ahead of him there were the roofs of native houses and what, as they advanced further, was a large village.

When they reached it the inhabitants stared at him, then looked quickly away.

He knew they were assuming he was Dutch, and had no wish to draw attention to themselves.

They walked on until they found what was obviously an open marketplace, and there, to the Duke's relief, he saw what he was seeking.

There were rickshaws, clumped together in a corner with

their owners squatting down and waiting for a chance customer.

It took the Duke a little time to explain that they wished to go to Jogyakarta.

He understood that the rickshaws of this village would only be prepared to carry him to the next.

There he would hire another to take him a few miles further on.

When at last it was understood what he wanted, there was a great deal of arguing over the price.

Although the Duke would have been prepared to pay anything that was asked, he had been too often in the Orient not to understand that half the fun of a transaction was the haggling which took place.

It would be extremely disappointing if an agreed solution was reached on both sides too quickly.

The Duke, as was expected, offered far less than he was actually prepared to pay, while the owner of the rickshaws named a price that was beyond his wildest dreams.

When finally agreement was reached, the Duke got into one rickshaw while Dawson took another.

They set off amid shouts and good wishes from the inhabitants of the village on what was obviously considered by them a long journey.

They must have travelled a quarter of the distance to Jogyakarta the first day, and they stayed the night in a house recommended by the rickshawmen.

It was primitive but clean, and the owners, while a little frightened of a white man, were as hospitable as it was possible for them to be.

The cottage was made of bamboo, thatched with materials which grew everywhere, and could be quickly constructed.

In the yard were chickens, ducks, dogs and pigs, mixed together with small children under coconut and banana trees.

All round the village there lay never-ending padi-fields, producing the rice which to the Javanese was the essence of life.

The food was exactly what the Duke had expected.

Coconut shells were used for ladles and bowls, while the fruit was grated to provide a rich creamy milk which was the basis for many of the meat and vegetable dishes.

As he was thirsty, he found the thin watery liquid made a refreshing drink.

There was fish which came from the rivers where the fishermen used large nets to catch them.

Because he was a foreigner, he and Dawson were served alone.

The children peeped at them, being made to wait for their meal until the guests had finished.

Their beds were on a slightly raised sleeping-platform where nets, pillows and bolsters were spread at night.

The Duke was tired and slept until dawn when once again they were on their way.

Three days later when they reached Jogyakarta, he had grown very tired of rice which was the basis of every meal he ate.

Fresh and dried fish and once a very tough chicken did little to relieve the monotony.

When they came to Jogyakarta he felt as if he had been travelling for years.

It was with a feeling of relief that having passed through the green crescent of rice lands he saw roofs, spires and domes.

The City was, Lord Curzon had told him, the centre of culture in Java.

It was, as the Duke had read in a guide-book of 1755, a sprawling city situated in the very core of an ancient region known as Mataram.

This had been the site of the first 8th century Javanese Empire.

From the 8th to the early 10th centuries it had been ruled over by a succession of Indian kings, the Buddhas, he was aware, of Borobudur.

It was impossible as he was carried through crowded streets not to feel excited.

When finally they reached the Royal Kraton, a two-centuries old Palace in the very heart of the City, he felt he had already achieved something momentous.

As he had expected, the Palace as was usual in the East, was not a single building, but a collection of pavilions with elegantly gilded pillars and beams.

There were ceremonial chambers, a magnificent Throne Hall, a Mosque and immense pleasure gardens.

He naturally did not see all this at once, but was taken through a maze of compounds to the private part of the Palace occupied by the Sultan.

He passed the front of the Throne Hall, which was an open pavilion consisting of a uniquely decorated and dramatically sloping roof supported in the centre by four massive wooden columns.

There was a strange mixture of crystal chandeliers and racoon furnishing in what otherwise was a classically Javanese setting.

He made it clear that he wished to wash and tidy himself before he met the Sultan.

He was taken to a typically Eastern room with however a beautiful 17th century paper on one of its walls.

There was also a Chinese picture which the Duke realised any connoisseur of art would welcome in his own collection.

He changed into fresh clothes, then informed the servant who was waiting outside his door that he was ready to see the Sultan.

Again he was led a very long distance down narrow corridors until he was escorted with a great deal of bowing from a vast number of servants into the presence of the Sultan himself.

Sultan Hamengku Buwono had inherited the throne in 1877 when he was 38, and now he was 50 and loved by his people.

A good looking man, he greeted the Duke effusively who expressed his pleasure at being in the Palace.

After the first greetings were over the attendants – and there seemed to be an army of them – withdrew.

The Sultan and the Duke were alone.

Then the older man led the way to two chairs standing in the very centre of the room.

For a moment the Duke was surprised.

Then he realised that that was a precaution so that, if they spoke in low voice, it would be impossible for anyone to overhear what was said.

He thought it was something which would amuse Lord Curzon and his eyes were twinkling when the Sultan indicated by a gesture of his hand that he should sit down.

He bowed, as was expected, to show his appreciation of the concession and sat opposite the Sultan.

They were near enough to one another so that not only could they not be overheard, but there was no possibility of their conversation being lip-read.

The Duke had heard from Lord Curzon the right way to address the Sultan was *Sinuhun* which means Highness.

"I bring, *Sinuhun Behi*, greetings from his Excellency," the Duke said in Javanese. "He regrets that he could not come himself in answer to your request for help."

"That His Excellency explained to me in the letter I received two days ago," the Sultan replied.

To the Duke's surprise he spoke in French and to explain why he went on:

"There is practically no-one in the Palace who speaks even a smattering of French, and I am sure, Sir, you are very fluent in that language. It makes what I have to say as safe from prying ears as it is possible for it to be."

"That I appreciate," the Duke murmured.

The Sultan gave a little laugh before he said:

"I can see, Sir, you are surprised that I should speak French, but when I was quite young I had a Concubine who was very beautiful. She taught me to speak French, being the daughter of a French sailor who had enjoyed her mother while his ship was in port at Jakarta."

The way he spoke was so amusing that the Duke laughed.

Then as if the two men understood each other the Sultan said:

"I am most grateful that you are here, but you understand it is of the utmost importance that the Dutch should have no idea why you are paying me a visit."

"I was told that by His Excellency when he learnt of what had happened to the treasures of Borobudur."

"It is something that has struck into the very heart of my people," the Sultan said. "We would all rather give our lives than have something like that happen to us again!"

"That I can understand," the Duke replied. "Do you, *Sinuhun* think now you have discovered another 'Borobudur'? It seems impossible!"

"From what I hear the Temple, or what we call a *Candi*, was built in about the 9th century."

"If that is true, it must be fantastic! Has Your *Sinuhun* seen it for yourself?"

The Sultan shook his head.

"No, that would be impossible, and for me to even show interest would encourage the Dutch either to pilfer from it or else to allow the thieves who are always searching for relics out of which they can make money to descend on it immediately!"

"Surely the Dutch must have some idea of the value to posterity of these ancient and magnificent buildings?" the Duke asked angrily.

The Sultan made an eloquent gesture with his hand, as he replied:

"Our conquerors are interested in only one thing and that is the money they can obtain for the products for which our people work unceasingly for little or no reward."

"It is intolerable!" the Duke exclaimed.

"That is how we feel," the Sultan agreed, "but if they do not work they starve. It is only because they have faith that one day, in this world or the next, their karma will be better that they can carry on."

The way the Sultan spoke was very moving.

The Duke was aware that to the Javanese their religion was more important than the accumulation of material wealth and gave them a hope that was unquenchable.

The Buddhists believed that they would take with them their religious merit into the next life.

For the Moslems their doctrine of accepting the word of Allah made them subservient to whatever was happening at the moment.

The Sultan however was explaining the reason why he had asked the Viceroy of India to help him.

"I have been told by somebody I trust," he said simply, "and who understands the necessity for secrecy that a certain *Candi* has been discovered a few miles away from here at Plaosan.

"And you were told it is unique?" the Duke asked.

The Sultan made his voice even lower than it had been before as he said:

"I am informed that Plaosan was build by a Shailendra Princess, a Buddhist, and her husband King Rakai Pikatan, who was the Hindu Ruler of Mataram."

55

The Duke's eyes widened as he realised that it was very unusual for a Temple to be built for two religions at the same time.

Yet there had been rumours that they existed in some parts of Java.

"If this is true," he said, "then archaeologically it will cause a great deal of excitement."

The Sultan instinctively glanced over his shoulder.

"That is something that must be avoided," he said.

"But why?"

"Because after the desecration of *Borobudur* the Elders of our people all over the country began to protest against the Dutch indifference to our treasured sites and to demand that something be done to preserve them."

"Do you think the Dutch will listen?" the Duke asked.

The Sultan made a gesture which was untranslatable in words.

"We can only hope and pray so," he replied. "At the same time, until they acknowledge some sort of responsibility it would be a risk to let them know that Plaosan exists."

"I can understand that," the Duke said, "and now Your Royal Highness must tell me exactly what you want me to do."

"Because I dare not trust any of my own people for fear that they will talk, and the Javanese are great talkers," the Sultan said with a smile, "I want you to verify that what I have heard is correct and try to make sure that nothing more is stolen while you are here."

"You are speaking as if something has been stolen already," the Duke said sharply.

"The reason why the information was brought to me in the first place," the Sultan explained, "was that somebody, and I do not think it was the Dutch in this case, has already taken away something very precious from the *Candi* and may of course take more."

The Duke thought with delight that it sounded as if there was much more to find.

He found himself not only intrigued, but longing to see what the Sultan was describing.

"What is important," the Sultan went on, "is that you should visit it casually, just as if you were looking round Jogyakarta not for Temples, but because you are a foreigner, and we are an interesting people."

"What Lord Curzon suggested," the Duke said, "is that I shall say if anybody asks me that I am writing an article on Java for the National Geographic Magazine. I expect you are aware that it is a very respected publication in England and in France."

"Yes, yes, of course," the Sultan replied, "it is a good idea. I imagine you have a camera?"

"I have," the Duke affirmed.

"They are very rare in Jogyakarta and it will certainly cause a sensation if you photograph the people in the streets, the children playing, or especially myself and the Palace."

"I will do all that," the Duke promised, "and as you yourself cannot visit Phaosan I will make sure that the pictures I take are handed to you secretly."

The Duke saw by the expression in the Sultan's eyes how the idea of this delighted him.

The Duke was very interested in photography and had taken some excellent pictures in India.

He owned one of the first Panorama Kodak Cameras which had been introduced the previous year. It covered an angle of 142°.

The photographs were really sensational and he seldom had a failure.

The Sultan, who seemed to be thinking deeply, said after a moment:

"I have another idea, one which I should enjoy myself and would give me very great pleasure."

"If there is anything I can do . . " the Duke began.

The Sultan leaned forward and was whispering against the Duke's ear as he said:

"I would like you to take photographs of my Concubines in the swimming-pool!"

For a moment the Duke was too astonished to reply.

He knew it was understood that a Concubine was hidden from the eyes of all men, except those of her master.

He thought with a smile that there were exceptions to every rule and he could understand the Sultan wished to have a memento of his favourites.

"I should be honoured to photograph anything or anybody Your *Sinuhun* suggests," he said.

There was no doubt that the Sultan was delighted.

"I have eighteen concubines," he said proudly, "and they are all very beautiful."

Later that night, after they had dined, they once again sat alone where they could not be overheard.

"If it suits you," the Sultan said, "I suggest you go early in the morning, soon after dawn to Plaosan."

"That is what I would like to do," the Duke said.

"I have one man I can trust to go with you. He is already in the secret because it was he in fact, who brought me the knowledge in the first place."

"He will ride with me?" the Duke asked.

"He will lead you there and you can trust him in anything you say."

The Duke thought this at any rate was a relief.

He was beginning to feel this 'hushed-up' attitude about everything would, in a few days, prove very trying.

"My *confidant's* name," the Sultan was saying, "Is Hadji. That is his first name. His second is very long, and very difficult to pronounce for anyone who is not Javanese."

"Hadji will suit me," the Duke smiled.

"Then tomorrow morning at half-after-five, he will be waiting for you," the Sultan said.

He rose as he spoke and the Duke realised he was dismissed.

He bowed and said in Javanese:

"Allah be with you!"

Then he went to his own room where Dawson was waiting for him.

"What do you make of it all, Dawson?" the Duke asked in a low voice. "Be careful what you say although I am certain only a few people here can speak English."

"It might be worse, Sir!" Dawson said laconically, "and the food's all right if you searches for it, so to speak. But I could do wiv a glass of ale!"

"Not in this household!" the Duke warned. "They are Moslems."

"I knows that," Dawson replied, "an' when I gets the chance I'll nip down into the town an' see what I can find."

The Duke, knowing Dawson, was quite certain he would find what he wanted.

He gave the man instructions to call him early in the morning and lay down.

The mattress was more comfortable than any he had slept on so far on the journey, and he almost instantly fell asleep.

It was still dark when the Duke was called and he dressed by candlelight.

Only as he stepped from the Palace into the courtyard was he aware that the sky was lightening.

He knew that as the dawn comes very quickly in the East, the light from the sun would soon be blinding.

Hadji, who was a small rather wizened little man of about the same age as the Sultan, was waiting for him.

He was very careful what he said until they had ridden out of the Palace and passed through the gates of the huge white wall.

This enclosed the Royal buildings, the pleasure-gardens and the Water Castle which was apparently fortified and surrounded on all four sides by a man-made lake.

The Duke however was not for the moment interested in the Palace, but in getting as quickly as he could to Plaosan.

The way the Sultan had described it last night made him feel that the object of his visit had an almost magnetic attraction for him.

He felt as if it was drawing him towards it in a way that he had never experienced before.

His body was responding to a force which he could not explain while his mind was activated in a way he did not understand.

He tried to tell himself that perhaps the whole thing was just a figment of his imagination and after they had gone a little further he said to Hadji:

"I understand it was you who notified the Sultan that this Temple exists."

"That is right, Sir. It was I who brought the news of it to the Palace."

"You are quite certain you are not mistaken in thinking it of great importance?"

Hadji smiled.

"Very soon you will see for yourself," he replied.

This prevented the Duke from asking any further questions, and they rode on, moving so quickly that it was impossible to converse.

Now the sun was rising and the small hamlets they passed were busy with workers setting off to the padi-fields and small children feeding the chickens.

Dogs barked and ran after them as they passed by.

They must have ridden for nearly an hour before Hadji

turned off the road which was little more than a track.

It was rough, uncultivated land, with many trees on it and a wood in the distance.

The Duke specially noticed two things: first a native cottage that seemed more solid than most of them on the left of their route.

Then when they reached the trees and moved slowly through them, ahead there was what appeared to be a very large hillock covered with climbing plants.

It was almost obscured by the trees surrounding it so that one could easily pass by without really noticing that it was there.

Hadji drew in his horse.

"I have somebody to see in the cottage," he said, "so I suggest, Sir, you go on and look at the *Candi*."

He dismounted as he spoke, and as the Duke did the same, Hadji took the bridle of his horse.

'I will look after him," he said.

Thinking that Hadji was being extremely tactful, the Duke walked over the rough ground.

As soon as he reached what he knew had to be the Temple, he took off his broad-brimmed hat and threw it down on the ground.

Because it was already very hot he also removed the light jacket he was wearing and laid it on the grass.

He undid his tie and opened the neck of his shirt a little way which left him feeling free and for the moment cool.

Quietly he moved forward to realise that what had been described as a *Candi* was far bigger than he had expected it to be.

He thought too, that while at first he had thought it to be round, he was sure on closer inspection that it was square.

Now amongst the rough overgrown grass there were stones which he was sure must have fallen from the roof and also, he suspected, from the galleries which ran round it.

He looked up but found it impossible to see anything through the vines of every sort and description which covered the great edifice.

It was very high, very wide, and he was quite certain that if it was cleared it would be a perfect square.

He looked in vain for the entrance, and as there appeared to be none he climbed over a number of the fallen stones until he reached what he knew must be the first gallery.

He was trying to find a foothold, being sure that if cleared the gallery would be wide.

If it was like other Temples he had seen or heard described, it would have sculpted reliefs running all round it.

These would start from the front, ending round the other side of it.

Moving carefully because the bricks at the edge of the gallery had fallen away from it, he started to work his way round the Temple.

He could only do so by holding onto the clinging vines.

Then as he turned the corner, he saw to his astonishment that he was not alone.

Standing on the gallery in the same way as he was, was a woman.

For a moment, because she was wearing a *sarong* he thought she was a native.

Then as she became aware of his presence she turned her face towards him.

He saw to his astonishment that her skin was white, and her hair which curled round her oval forehead was very fair.

As he looked at her he realised that she was very lovely; in fact one of the most beautiful women he had ever seen.

It flashed through his mind that he must either be dreaming or seeing a vision.

Perhaps she was just a ghost of the Shailendra Princess who was responsible for the *Candi* itself.

To his astonishment the woman's eyes widened as she stared at him.

Then, obviously equally astonished, she asked in English:

"Are you . . real?"

Chapter Four

The Duke was too surprised to reply, and the girl asked:

"Why are you . . here?"

There was a look of fear in her large eyes, and the Duke said cautiously:

"I think I should ask you that question."

Now she looked at him in surprise and he said:

"Are you a tourist like myself?"

She did not answer, but reached out her hand and pulled some vines over the wall beside her.

It was then the Duke had an idea and he asked:

"Do you perhaps live in that cottage which I saw a short distance away?"

There was a definite expression of what was almost terror now in her eyes as she answered:

"I do not . . think that has . . anything to do . . with you . . !"

"I just wondered if the man who guided me here and has now gone to the cottage wanted perhaps to see you," the Duke remarked.

Now there was a very different expression in the girl's eyes as she stared at him.

He knew instinctively that she was wondering if she could trust him or if in fact, he was an enemy.

Then she asked hesitatingly in a very low voice:

"Are . . you . . Dutch?"

The Duke smiled.

"We are speaking English, and I am as English as I imagine you are!"

She gave a deep sigh and said:

"If you are a tourist . . I cannot think why . . "

She stopped, then after a second added:

"What is the name of the man who brought you here?"

"His name is Hadji."

She gave a cry that was so obviously one of relief that the Duke said:

'You can trust me, and I promise you faithfully, I will not do you or anything else any harm."

He looked at the vine-covered wall beside him as he spoke, and the girl said again hesitatingly:

"Has somebody . . sent you?"

"That is a question which I think you should ask your friend Hadji."

"Then you . . come from . . the Sultan!"

She whispered the words as if she was terrified to say them, but had to know the truth.

The Duke smiled at her.

"Now I suggest we start from the beginning and introduce ourselves," he said. "I am a tourist interested in photographing the wonders of Java and my name is Bury."

He paused, but he knew instinctively that she was waiting for him to continue, and he said very quietly:

"I was told that there is something here which should be recorded by my camera."

"Now I . . understand," the girl cried, "and thank you . . thank you for . . coming!"

She spoke with such enthusiasm and anxiety that the Duke was aware how much it meant to her.

"Now that I have introduced myself," he said, "I am waiting to hear your name."

"It is Sarida."

There was a little pause and the Duke said:

"A Javanese name for an English girl. That is unusual."

"My father chose it specially."

"And your father's name?"

"M. Martin."

The Duke smiled.

"Now we are properly introduced and I should be grateful, Miss Martin, to know what all this is about."

She clasped her hands together and the sunshine coming through the thick boughs of the trees turned her hair to gold.

"Is it . . true," she asked, "really true that you . . have come to help . . where it is most . . needed?"

"I am hoping to do that," the Duke said, "but you will have to explain to me what I can do."

He thought she was still hesitating and he said:

"Perhaps it will make things easier if I tell you that I am already aware that this *Candi* is unique."

"You know it is a *Candi*?" she asked in a very low voice.

"That is what I have been told."

Again she gave a deep sigh.

"Then only the Sultan could have told you that . . and I have been praying . . desperately that he would find . . somebody to prevent the Dutch and the . . thieves from ruining what is holy . . and very . . very . . wonderful!"

"That is what I want to see," the Duke said.

He thought she was about to move, and he added:

"But first, tell me why you asked when you saw me if I was real?"

Now there was definitely a hint of laughter in Sarida's eyes and the smile on her perfect lips was somehow mischievous.

Yet still she hesitated and he knew once again she was afraid that she was making a mistake.

"You must understand," the Duke said, "that I am extremely curious."

Sarida gave a little laugh, and reaching out, she pulled aside the vines on the wall beside which she was standing.

Behind them there was a relief carved on the wall, which the Duke saw had been cleaned.

When he looked at it he realised it must be of King Rakai Pikatan who had built the *Candi* with his wife.

It was exquisitely carved.

Then as Sarida moved more of the vines away and he could see the King's face which was hardly damaged at all, it seemed vaguely familiar.

Then as he looked at it he realised incredulously that it was the same face he saw every time he looked in a mirror, in fact his own.

He stared at the relief thinking he must be mistaken, then Sarida asked:

"Now you understand why I thought when I first saw you that you were a ghost, or perhaps a vision from the past!"

The Duke remembered that he had felt the same about her, but thought it would be a mistake to say so.

Instead he stared at the relief of the King and put out his hand to touch the stone very carefully.

The relief had been broken just below the waist, but he had the idea that if they searched on the gallery, the piece would come to light.

"Did you find this?" he asked, knowing that Sarida was waiting for him to speak.

"I found the *Candi*," she said, "and I thought when I had done so that nobody knew of it except me."

"And what did you intend to do about it?" the Duke asked.

"I thought as it had been hidden for so long that there was no fear of the Dutch finding it. As you know, they are not interested in the treasures of Java."

The Duke knew without words that she was thinking of the way they had behaved at Borobudur.

"Then," Sarida went on, "something . . terrible . . happened!"

'What was that?" he asked.

"The Lord Buddha in the . . chamber inside was . . stolen."

The Duke looked at her in astonishment.

"You have been inside?"

"Yes, of course. I do not know how it happened, but one day the Lord Buddha with the two Bodhisattvas on either side of him, were there and the . . next day . . he had . . gone!"

"Who do you think took him?"

Sarida made a helpless little gesture.

"How can we know the truth?" she asked. "Actually I think it was one of the thieves who, when they became aware that the treasures in Borobudur were priceless enough to be presented to the King of Siam, have been seeking for *Candis* from which they can steal their treasures and sell them."

The Duke frowned.

"It is intolerable!" he said.

"It is heart-breaking!" Sarida answered. "This beautiful wonderful *Candi*, which has existed since the 9th century . . is now being . . pilfered and Java . . deprived of something which is of . . inestimable value!"

"I agree with you," the Duke said, "but I am not certain what can be done about it."

"The Sultan hoped that the Viceroy of India, Lord Curzon, might be able to help."

"That is why I am here," the Duke said.

"Then he has responded to the Sultan's plea! Oh, thank you, thank you for coming!"

She spoke so earnestly that the Duke could not help thinking it was extraordinary that she minded so much.

Why should she, an English girl, be so concerned with the heritage of Java?

There were many questions he wanted to ask, but first he thought he should see where the Buddha had been.

"What I would like to do," he said, "is to enter this strange building, if you will show me the way."

She smiled and said:

"I will do that, but first we have to retrace our steps, as the gallery is broken further along. Be careful how you move or you might fall and hurt yourself."

As she spoke she started to pull the vines over the relief of the King to hide it, as it must have been hidden for centuries.

It seemed extraordinary, he thought, that the King's face was almost a replica of his own.

He knew that later he would want to come back and look at the relief again to make quite sure that neither he nor Sarida were imagining the resemblance.

Very carefully, as he had no wish to fall, he retraced his steps until as they turned round a corner of the building he thought they must be at the front.

He was not mistaken, and Sarida climbed over the fallen stones again moving the hanging vines.

Now the Duke could see that in what he imagined was the centre of the wall there was a large opening, but the vines made it possible to enter the building only if they crawled.

"Let me go first," Sarida said. "I have a lantern inside which I will light, and you will be able to see clearly what is . . missing."

There was a little sob in her voice as she said the last word.

Then moving forward she crawled beneath the vines and disappeared.

The Duke waited, thinking this was the most extraordinary encounter and certainly one he had not expected.

His curiosity was aroused, and he knew he must find out why Sarida, so young and so lovely, should be concerned with a Buddhist Temple.

He wanted to know why she was living in the cottage, in what appeared to be an uninhabited and uncultivated part of the country.

There were a dozen more questions he wanted answered.

But he knew that more important than anything else was that he should see if Sarida was correct in her assumption that this Temple was unique.

Then as he stood there thinking, he heard her say in a soft, low voice:

"You can come in, but be careful because the ground is very rough."

As she had done, the Duke went under the hanging vines on his knees.

Inside he found as he expected that the Temple was divided into three compartments.

In the centre one, which was very high and he found he could stand up in it, was the altar of Buddha.

The lantern Sarida had lit was quite a large one and there was also some light coming from an opening high up on the wall near the roof.

The light was faint, but it revealed quite clearly that between the two massive figures of the Bodhissatvas was the throne on which the Buddha had sat.

The Bodhissatvas that flanked him were exquisitely carved. In fact, the Duke had never before seen such beautiful and well-preserved statues.

He could understand the agony it must have been for Sarida to know that where the Buddha had sat was now just an empty stone.

As if she was following his thoughts, Sarida said in a low voice:

"He was very beautiful! I shall never forget the . . serenity of his . . face and the way he . . seemed to . . vibrate towards . . me."

She spoke in a rapt little voice.

Looking down the Duke could now see there were joss-sticks on the floor and as in most Buddhist Temples, there was a bowl filled with sand into which the joss-sticks were put after the worshippers had lit them.

He was aware now of the scent of incense in the Temple, and he guessed that Sarida had not only lit joss-sticks, but had also come here to pray.

He was aware she was praying now with her eyes on the spot where the statue of Buddha had once been, and he knew that inwardly she was seeing him in her mind.

He moved a little nearer to one of the Bodhisattvas, whose leg was crossed in the familiar position, his head turned towards the Buddha.

He felt a sudden anger that the three figures which had survived for so long should now have been desecrated.

The two chambers on either side were filled with rubble and soil because the roof had fallen in and left holes above them.

He had the idea that they too would have contained a Buddha with his two Bodhisattvas.

He decided then that any further theft from this Temple must be prevented at all costs.

As if she knew what he was thinking, Sarida said:

"I think we should . . talk about it . . outside."

The way she spoke told the Duke that the place was sacred to her, and she thought even a discussion on how to protect it would somehow spoil the atmosphere.

He moved towards the entrance, and as he reached it Sarida extinguished the lantern.

As he looked back he saw her kneel down in front of the empty space where the Buddha had been.

Her fingers were pressed together in the age-old attitude, which was both that of Christian prayer and the Oriental gesture of greeting and respect.

Then as she bowed her head he thought it very touching that she should pray to the god who was hardly known to the English.

The Buddha's divine and deeply erudite teaching had been supplanted even in Java by the Moslem faith.

He went out of the Temple and waited for several minutes before Sarida joined him.

There was an expression in her eyes which he thought he had not seen often on any woman's face, and was one he could only describe as spiritual.

It was as if her prayers had swept her away from the mundane world into a Heaven where he could not reach her.

He could not explain what he was feeling even to himself, and yet he was vividly aware of her as she came towards him.

Without speaking they moved down over the tumbled stones to ground level.

Then Sarida led the way to where there was a fallen tree and sat down on it, looking back to where the great pile looked once again like a hillock.

"What can you . . do about . . it?" she asked.

The Duke knew it was a question of deep significance.

"It is everything, and more, that has been described to me."

"You are sure of . . that?" she asked.

He smiled.

"I think you know better than I do that it is a perfect example of the exquisite architecture of the 9th century, and certainly unique in showing a very unusual religious tolerance.'

He saw the delight on Sarida's face as she said:

"I will show you a relief of the Shailendra Princess who you know was a Buddhist, and you have already seen her husband."

The Duke did not speak, and after a moment she asked:

"How is it . . possible that you resemble him so . . closely that when I first saw you I . . thought I must be . . dreaming?"

She spoke as a child might have done, and the Duke was aware that she was not being in the slightest flirtatious.

He knew she was not thinking of him, as many women had done, as an attractive man whom they desired.

To her he was the King and he knew before she said it, what she was thinking.

"Perhaps," she said in such a soft voice that he could hardly hear her, "it was you who ordered this Temple to be built, and I have the idea, although I may be wrong, that there is another not far distant from it, and also a *Stupa*."

"Are you sure of that?" the Duke asked eagerly.

"Almost sure, but they are much damaged. The stones are sunk into the ground and have been covered with so many plants and foliage that it would be impossible for me to move any of them, and it would be a mistake for me to employ anybody to do so."

"Yes, of course," the Duke agreed.

Then after a little silence, he said:

"Let us get back to the original question of what can be done."

"Where are you staying?" Sarida asked unexpectedly.

"I am a guest of the Sultan, and you will understand that officially he is interested in me merely because I have an up-to-date camera, and have promised to show him my photographs of Jogyakarta."

"That is clever," Sarida said, "and no one will be suspicious wherever you travel or take photographs.'

"That is what His Royal Highness thought," the Duke

said, "but I see I must be very careful."

Sarida was silent, then she said:

"If you are staying at the Palace, it is difficult for me to say what I was going to suggest if anybody came here from India, as I have been hoping."

"What was your idea?" the Duke enquired.

She looked away from him towards the *Candi* as she said:

"You may think I am just being imaginative, but it is about four weeks since the Buddha was stolen, and I have the idea that the thieves will soon return."

"Why should you think that?" the Duke enquired.

She made a helpless little gesture with her hand before she said:

"You will not believe me, but I was told that would happen when I was . . praying inside . . the Temple."

The Duke thought that was the answer he might have expected.

"I do believe you," he said, "and I will therefore come and stay here at night, as soon as you ask me to do so."

Sarida gave a little cry.

"Do you . . mean that? Do you . . really . . mean it?"

"Of course I mean it," the Duke answered, "and I hope, as I believe it is the rainy season, I shall not have to spend too many nights underneath the trees!"

Sarida gave a little laugh.

"That will be unnecessary. We can see the wood quite clearly from the cottage, and it would be impossible for any one man to carry away a statue alone."

She looked at the Duke before she went on and said:

"After the Lord Buddha was gone I looked for cart-tracks but there were none. Yet I feel sure that if they come here again they will follow the route you used over firm ground."

The Duke realised that she was talking good sense.

He and Hadji had ridden over high ground before they reached the woods.

He remembered now that it had sloped away into a swamp which because, as he had said, it was the rainy season, looked almost like a lake.

He was sure Sarida was right in thinking that the thieves would bring a cart right up to the edge of the wood.

They would then only have a comparatively short distance through the trees to carry the statue before they could drive away with it.

Then no-one except those living in the cottage would be aware of their visit.

The more he thought about it, the more he was sure that Sarida was right in thinking they would come back.

The two Bodhisattvas were exquisitely carved, and he was almost certain that if the rubble was cleared in the two adjacent chambers there would be found three statues in each.

All of which would be extremely valuable to the Connoisseurs.

Aloud he said:

"It will be quite easy for me to tell the Sultan, or anyone else who is interested, that I want to take some photographs at night. With a full moon they should develop clearly enough for me to explain why I am taking photographs after dark."

He saw the joy in Sarida's eyes, but before she could speak he went on:

"All you have to tell me is exactly, if that is possible, when we may expect our unwelcome visitors. If I can do nothing else, perhaps I could frighten them so that they will look elsewhere for their spoils."

"Thank you, thank you!" Sarida said. "I promise I will try not to be a tremendous . . nuisance to . . you."

"You will not be that," the Duke said, "and as you can imagine, I want to take photographs which I can show the Viceroy, and also the Sultan."

"Be careful," Sarida said quickly, "not to let anybody else see them."

"I promise you I will not endanger this wonderful building more than it is at risk already."

"It is so wonderful that you are here," Sarida said.

She spoke as if a heavy burden had been taken from her shoulders.

"You must help me by getting enough lanterns or lights of some sort," the Duke said, "so that I can photograph the Bodhisattvas perhaps tomorrow morning."

"I think first we should speak to Hadji," Sarida said. "You will understand that, because you are staying at the Palace, people will be very curious about you. In case they ask where you have been you must visit other places besides this."

The Duke nodded.

"I understand, and now shall we go back to your cottage and talk to Hadji?"

She rose eagerly as if she wanted to do everything very quickly.

The Duke picked up his coat, his tie and his hat from where he had thrown them down.

Carrying them over his arm he walked through the trees onto the open ground.

The cottage was only a short distance away. He now saw it was larger than he had thought when he had first seen it.

The garden around it was filled with flowers, and he thought it looked very attractive.

"How long have you lived here?" he asked.

"Only for six months. We came here from Siam," Sarida explained.

"Siam?" the Duke repeated in surprise.

He was just about to ask her why she was so interested in Oriental countries when she explained:

"Papa is writing a book on Buddhism. It is a subject in which he is absorbedly interested, and we have already been to the Lord Buddha's birthplace in India, and have visited the glorious Temples to him in Siam."

"Has your father written many books?" the Duke enquired.

"Only two others on Oriental religions."

The Duke tried to remember if he had ever read any books by somebody called 'Martin', but the name did not ring a bell.

"Papa is not very well," Sarida explained, "and because it would upset him, I have not told him about the Lord Buddha being stolen."

The Duke was surprised.

"He has not seen the empty space in the Temple?"

"Papa has been confined to the house for the last two months. He writes, but he gets very tired, and I had hoped to persuade him earlier in the year that we should go home to England."

"Where do you live?" the Duke asked.

"In Buckinghamshire."

With difficulty the Duke prevented himself from saying that was the County where his house was situated.

Again he tried to remember if he had ever heard of anyone called Martin.

After a moment's pause he asked:

"Whereabouts in Buckinghamshire?"

"Not far from Aylesbury," Sarida said.

The Duke was even more surprised, but it was impossible for him to say so.

He was quite certain that Sarida would have heard of him.

By this time they had reached the garden.

As she went ahead of him, moving with a grace that he had admired in Indian women, he thought if she appeared in the Social World she would cause a sensation.

Sarida opened the door of the cottage which was larger and better built than those in which he had stayed on his journey from the coast.

At the same time it was a typical Javanese house with a thatched roof.

Inside, to his surprise, while the ceilings were low, there were some exquisite Eastern rugs on the floors.

Although the furniture was obviously made by local craftsmen, it was very attractive.

As they entered the Sitting-Room which was larger than the Duke had expected, Hadji, who was sitting by a couch on which reclined an elderly man, rose to his feet.

Sarida ran towards him.

"How lovely to see you!" she said in Javanese. "And thank you for bringing Mr. Bury."

Hadji looked at the Duke with a question in his eyes.

"It is magnificent," the Duke said, "and must be preserved at all costs!"

The expression in Hadji's eyes was very touching.

"That is what I hoped you would say, Sir."

"I am waiting for you to meet my father," Sarida said at the Duke's side.

He walked to the couch which was drawn up by the window.

Lying back against a number of pillows was a very distinguished looking man.

He was quite obviously English, and as Sarida had spoken to the Duke in that language, he looked up in surprise.

"Mr. Bury is English, Papa," Sarida explained, "and he has come in response to the Sultan's letter to the Viceroy."

"That is very kind of you," her father said holding out his hand.

"It is a great privilege," the Duke said, "to see anything so remarkable, and in such a fine state of preservation."

He thought as he spoke of the two Bodhisattvas and also the relief of the King which resembled himself.

"I am sure you will understand, Mr. Bury," Sarida's father said, "that it is a crime that these ancient and magnificent Temples should be ignored by the Dutch and ransacked of their treasures, as Borobudur was."

"I have only recently learned what happened," the Duke replied, "and like the Viceroy I am appalled at such vandalism."

"You can imagine how we feel!" Hadji said in Javanese. "We love our country, and it is agonising to realise how little our traditions mean to our conquerors."

The pain in his voice was something which the Duke thought must be felt by every intelligent Javanese.

A servant brought them coffee and some delicious small cakes which were so English that the Duke was sure that Sarida had made them.

They sat talking for a while, until as Mr. Martin looked tired Hadji rose to his feet.

"I think we should go back to the City," he said to the Duke.

"I must first have a word with Miss Sarida," he replied.

She understood and together they walked from the room and out into the garden.

"I will not come to you tonight," he said, "unless you think it is urgent that I should do so, but I will come early tomorrow morning. I hope in the meantime you can arrange something about lighting in the Temple."

"I will do my best," Sarida replied.

"Who else lives here?" the Duke enquired.

"We have three servants who all belong to one family. They are a simple people, and they ask no questions. They are only frightened of the Dutch."

"Then you do not think they will talk?"

Sarida smiled.

"To whom?" she asked looking out over the wasteland where there was not a house in sight.

"I see your point!" the Duke smiled. "But I think you should be very careful and for Heaven's sake, if you think there are thieves approaching the Temple, do not interfere with them!"

"It will be difficult not to do so! However they must be very experienced because when they came before I did not hear them and Papa sleeps very lightly."

"Promise me that you will do nothing foolish," the Duke said. "Remember you are young and alive, and what you are protecting has been dead for a long time!"

He spoke without thinking.

Then as he saw the expression on Sarida's face he realised that to her the statues in the Temple were as alive and breathing as she was herself.

They were a part of the mystic world where she went in her prayers, and he knew that compared to that the body she inhabited at the moment was of no significance.

Quite suddenly the idea of her being hurt or injured, perhaps even killed, made him angry.

"You must promise me to do as I say," he said, "and not take any unnecessary risks. If you do not promise, I shall go away, and not come back!"

She stared at him. Then she said with a little smile:

"I think, Mr. Bury, you are blackmailing me!"

"If I am, it is for your own good," he replied. "You are not living in the quiet and peace of the English countryside, but in a land that can be very dangerous!"

"A land which hundreds and thousands of Javanese have died to defend!" Sarida murmured softly.

"But you are not Javanese."

"I feel, because they mean so much to Papa, that I am part of them," she said.

"Nevertheless," the Duke replied, "you must give me your promise on everything you hold sacred."

He put out his hand as he spoke and almost as if he forced her to do so, she put her hand in his.

His fingers closed over it and he felt a little tremor go through her as if she was afraid and, like a captured bird, wished to escape from him.

"Promise!" he insisted.

For a moment she hesitated, then she said:

"I promise . . but please . . come to me if I call . . for you."

"I swear I will do that," the Duke answered.

For a moment he looked into her eyes and knew she was searching his face for reassurance that he was completely sincere.

Then Hadji came out to join them, and the Duke released her hand.

As the Duke rode away he thought that never in his life had he had a more strange encounter, or found such an exquisite Temple.

Neither had he seen a girl as beautiful as Sarida.

How was it possible, he asked himself, that she should be living alone with her ill father?

She was apparently happy, as no other woman could have been, because she was immersed in a mystic world that he could not completely comprehend

He felt it would be difficult even to make George Curzon realise how strange it was and how unexpected.

Then as he rode on, good practical common sense made him take photographs of a village through which they were passing.

There were women washing the clothes in the swollen streams, children playing beneath the banana trees, while two small boys were trying to climb them.

*

The Duke was not surprised when he arrived back at the Palace to find that the Sultan wished to see him and that he should bring his camera with him.

He was sitting in one of the beautiful open pavilions and the Duke took photographs of him there, then more in the pleasure gardens.

After luncheon when the Duke had eaten a variety of Javanese dishes he had never sampled before, the Sultan had a suggestion to make.

Speaking in French so that no one else could understand he told his guest he was taking him to the Bathing Pool.

The Duke was not quite sure what he expected.

Certainly nothing as attractive as the impressive entrance through very high white walls, leading to a large round central pool with a naga-head fountain.

There was a pavilion at one end of it and the Sultan, manoeuvring the Duke towards it, explained that the pool at which he was looking was designed to be used by his Concubines.

Inside the pavilion a staircase took them up to a small, well-furnished room.

There were windows overlooking the central pool and others onto a small pool on the other side of the Pavilion which the Sultan explained was exclusively his.

The chamber which was high up above the central pool was where he rested in the afternoon.

From there he could watch his Harem disport themselves in the clear water under the spray of the fountain.

"No one will know you are here, my friend," he said to the Duke. "So you can take your photographs through the open window, and I will be waiting impatiently to see them!"

The Sultan then lay down on a couch while the Duke set up his camera so that it pointed down to the circular pool.

He thought afterwards that no-one would believe he had

had such an unusual and special privilege.

The Concubines ran naked into the water looking like graceful butterflies.

They had flowers and jewels in their hair, and they threw down on the parapet surrounding the pool the brilliantly coloured cloaks which had covered their bodies.

Some of them were very young, but all of them had a beauty that the Duke thought would be difficult to capture even with a camera.

In a low voice the Sultan explained to him where each girl came from.

There were several Chinese, two Siamese, and an exquisite creature who looked as if she must have stepped out of a painted fan and came from Japan.

The rest were Javanese.

The Duke thought that no man could look at them without being moved with an irresistible desire to possess such loveliness.

Then strangely, while he was photographing them, one after another, he found himself thinking of Sarida, of her white skin and golden hair.

Her eyes, which strangely were not blue, but the green flecked with gold of a mountain stream, seemed to haunt her.

He was sure that her body was as exquisitely formed as that of a Green goddess.

He found himself hoping that the Sultan would never see her, lest she should be added to his collection.

Then he told himself he should concentrate on the job in hand.

Yet now, in some strange way, the women did not seem as lovely as they had at first, and he was no longer moved by their nakedness.

Chapter Five

After the Duke had gone Sarida searched the house for lights by which he could photograph the Temple.

There was an oil-lamp in her father's room by which he wrote which she thought she could borrow at the last moment.

There was another which they used in the Sitting-Room and some small ones in the bedrooms.

She hoped that when she arranged them inside the dark chamber the Duke would have enough light to get good photographs of the Bodhisattvas.

It broke her heart to think that if only he had come earlier he would have been able to photograph the Lord Buddha before he was stolen away.

She had often lain awake since it had happened, wondering how she had not been awakened by the noise of wheels passing the cottage on the way to the wood.

Moreover, because what served as a rough track was stony, she should have heard the horses' hoofs.

Sometimes in her fantasies she thought the Buddha had been taken away not by human hands, but he had returned to another world where she could reach him only by prayer.

Then she was terrified that if the thieves came again they would take the two Bodhisattvas.

Perhaps they would also find in the two other chambers treasures she had not yet been able to discover.

Now, as if it was inevitable, her thoughts turned to Mr.

Bury and she asked herself over and over again how it was possible he should look exactly like the builder of the Temple.

Thinking that perhaps she was imagining the resemblance, she climbed again onto the gallery and pulled aside the vines to look at the relief of the King.

Then she knew that he certainly did look very like the Englishman.

She was of course, thinking of him as an ordinary man, and it crossed her mind that he must have behaved very badly in one of his lives to have been reborn into such a lowly position after having been a King.

"I wonder what he did," she pondered.

She thought because he was so handsome that his sins must somehow be connected with women.

Because she spent most of her time with her father and talked of little but the great Oriental religions in which he was so interested, she was very innocent and ignorant about the Social World.

She was aware that if her mother had been alive she would last year have had a Season in London and made her curtsy to the Queen, or to the Prince of Wales and his wife.

She would of course, have attended the Balls which were the 'El Dorado' of every debutante.

But because she knew nothing about London Society she did not miss it.

She was in fact content to learn the strange customs of the countries in which they had stayed, and to meet in India a wide variety of different people, from Maharajas to men and women of the lowest caste.

She found them absorbingly interesting.

She also found beauty everywhere she looked, from the Temples and Palaces of India to the great river of Siam.

She loved the smiling faces of the Siamese, who always seemed happy and the friendliness of the Javanese touched her whenever she encountered it.

"I am so lucky!" she had often said to herself. "I have everything!"

Yet now that she had met Mr. Bury she knew that because of King Rakai Pikatan his face had always been in her dreams.

It made her feel different from how she had ever felt before and she could not explain it to herself.

She only knew that the moment he had appeared on the gallery of the Temple she had been vividly aware of him as she had never been of any other man.

When he had held her hand closely in his and made her promise she would not interfere with the thieves, she had felt something strange within her heart.

Even after he had left it did not go away.

She wanted to talk to her father and ask him if he thought it possible that Mr. Bury was a reincarnation of King Rakai Pikatan.

Then she remembered that her father must not know there was any trouble in the Temple because it would distress him.

He was too ill to be worried.

She could remember only too vividly how furious he had been when he first learned of the way in which the Dutch had looted Borobudur.

It had made him too weak to write for several days.

Because she wanted to be near him she went into his room where he was already in bed, but still writing his manuscript.

"How much have you written today, Papa?" she asked sitting down beside him.

"Not as much as I would like," he replied, "but my book is nearly finished."

"That is wonderful!" Sarida exclaimed.

"Then we will go home," her father said. "It is time we

opened the house and remembered that we are English."

Sarida laughed.

"I never forget that," she said, "at the same time, I know your book will be an inspiration to everybody who reads it."

"I can only hope so," her father said in a tired voice.

He looked at his daughter as he spoke and after a moment he said:

"Perhaps I was wrong to take you away for so long from your rightful background. You are very beautiful, my dear, as a great many Englishmen will tell you when we return."

Sarida remembered there was one Englishman now who admired her, but she thought it a mistake to say so.

Her father leaned back against his pillows.

"As soon as I have finished my book we will return," he said firmly.

His eyes were closed and Sarida knew he was talking more to himself than to her.

Very gently she took the manuscript off the bed and extinguished the light.

When she left the room she knew her father had not heard her go.

In the morning Sarida rose early as she felt the Englishman would come soon after dawn.

She was not mistaken, and when she saw him riding towards the cottage, she felt her heart leap with excitement.

He was alone, not accompanied by Hadji, and she ran out to greet him.

He dismounted thinking as he looked at Sarida that she was even lovelier than she had been the day before.

The first light of dawn seemed to linger on her hair and he thought she was so very different from any other woman that he knew it was impossible to put it into words.

"I think," Sarida said in her soft voice, "you should put your horse in the shed at the back of the cottage. It would be a mistake for anybody to see him and think perhaps that you have come from the Palace."

The Duke was aware that the horse he was riding was superior to those he had passed on the road, or could be seen moving about the City.

He therefore thought this was a sensible suggestion and led the horse to a rough shed where there was a manger and a bucket of water ready for him.

Then carrying his camera he went back to where Sarida was waiting.

"I have put all the lights that we have in the Temple," she said, "and I am hoping they will be enough."

"Then let us do that first," the Duke suggested, "before there is any chance of anybody being about."

They walked towards the Temple.

As they moved through the trees, the Duke noticed for the first time there were clumps of stones covered in moss or grasses, winding away into the distance.

He told himself that he must find out if it was true, as Sarida suspected, that another *Candi* had stood nearby and if she was right in believing there was also a *Stupa*.

As if he felt he was going too fast, he told himself severely 'First things first', and went down on his knees to follow Sarida into the Temple.

One by one she lit the lights and when she had finished the Duke was certain he would be able to get a good photograph of each of the Bodhisattvas.

Like Sarida, he deeply regretted that he had not been able to come sooner, when the Buddha was still there.

He took a number of exposures, thinking as he did so that what he was photographing now was very different from those the Sultan had requested yesterday.

He had left Dawson at the Palace developing them.

He had taken a great deal of trouble last night preparing a dark-room in which they could be developed and printed.

He had immediately become interested in photography when some years earlier the first cameras appeared to excite the public.

He had set up a dark-room at his house in Buckinghamshire, because he found it annoying to have to wait sometimes for weeks before his films could be professionally developed and returned to him.

He had been taught by one of the experts at Kodak, and he in his turn had taught Dawson.

This meant that on their travels, especially in India, he did not have to spend hours in a hot, airless dark-room when he might be outside taking more pictures.

He had become very proficient as a photographer and he was extremely flattered when his work was commended by experts.

He had already filled several albums with photographs, and guests who stayed with him at Ingle Castle would pore over them with great interest.

Naturally the women who were in love with him asked for his photograph.

They also insisted that he take theirs, which they fondly hoped he would keep close to his heart.

He was, however, more interested in his artistic ability to produce what he thought was a good portrait rather than ready to enthuse over the subject itself.

Yet now as he took one exposure after another of the Bodhisattvas, he found himself thinking that he must photograph Sarida.

He was quite certain that when he had done so her portrait would rival, if not excel, those he had already taken of the 'Marlborough House Beauties'.

'She is wasted here in Java,' he thought.

Then he told himself it would be a mistake to become too

involved however lovely she was.

But when they emerged from the Temple out into the sunshine he found it impossible not to look at her and go on looking.

She was wearing a green sarong and it made her body seem part of the trees, the grass and the flowers.

Yet her face might have been carved with the same exquisite delicacy as the Bodhisattvas and, he thought, as the reliefs.

On an impulse he put down his camera on a stone and said:

"You have not yet shown me a sculpture of the Princess. I cannot believe that she is not somewhere on the gallery."

"Yes, of course," Sarida answered, "but she is smaller than the King, as would be expected, and tucked away rather coyly beside him, because of course, being a man he was more important than she was!"

There was a provocative little note in her voice which made the Duke laugh.

"Show me the Shailendra Princess, and I will see if she is as beautiful as I expect."

He climbed along the gallery, Sarida leading the way.

When they came to the relief of the King, she pulled back the vines so that he could see once again his own face.

He had convinced himself during the night that he must have been mistaken, or perhaps hypnotised in some way by Sarida into thinking that there was any real resemblance.

But now when he looked again at the relief, there could be no doubt even in the most sceptical observer, that the King's face was like his own.

It would be absurd to dispute it.

Then as Sarida pulled aside more vines he saw that beside the King there was a sculpture of the Princess.

It was very much smaller than that of the King, and in this case too the stone had been very little damaged.

In fact, her face might have been chiselled only a year or so ago.

The Duke looked at it, and Sarida waited for his comment, her eyes on his face.

He looked at the relief and thought that once again he was seeing what he had half-expected rather than what was actually there.

He even shut his eyes as if to focus them better, but the carving did not move or alter. It was, although he fought against admitting it, very like Sarida.

Because what he was seeing perturbed him, he said almost roughly:

"I presume you are expecting me to take a photograph of this?"

"I certainly think you should take the King," Sarida replied.

The Duke was frowning as he went back to get his camera.

Was he dreaming? Was he being tricked?

How was it possible that he should come to Java and find a replica of himself, and beside it one of the girl now living centuries after the original sculpture had been made?

It flashed through his mind that perhaps somebody was deceiving him.

Perhaps it was all an absurd hoax thought up by the Sultan to draw attention to what was happening in Jogyakarta.

Then he knew that was impossible.

However much he might fight against admitting it, the reliefs sculpted in the 9th century depicted himself and Sarida.

He took the photographs, and when he had done so Sarida without making any comment pulled the vines back into place.

Even if anybody passing through the wood was aware

that the hillock was there, they would not see anything to make them think it was extraordinary or different from the land around it.

Slowly, walking side by side, they went back towards the cottage.

Only when they were half-way there did the Duke say somewhat harshly:

"Have you any explanation for what you have just shown me?"

"I think you know the answer to . . that," Sarida said very quietly.

"Are you really expecting me to believe in reincarnation, in what the Buddhists called the 'Wheel of Rebirth'?" the Duke demanded.

She did not reply, but he knew the answer without her saying it.

Because he could read her thoughts it made him in a way more aggressive than he was already.

The truth was that he was afraid of what he did not understand.

Because it was new to him, and because there was no plausible or easy explanation, he did not want to think of it.

As if Sarida understood that it was himself he was annoyed with, when they reached the cottage she said:

"When you have had breakfast, I am sure Papa would like to see you."

The Duke hesitated.

He wanted to stay – at the same time he wanted to go away.

He could not understand his own feelings, except that he was perturbed by them.

As he hesitated Sarida looked over his shoulder, then gave a little exclamation.

"What is it?" he asked.

He turned his head as he spoke and saw in the far

distance, coming from the same direction as he had, three men on horseback.

"Who are they?" he asked.

"The Dutch!" Sarida said. "Quick! They must not find you here!"

She moved inside the cottage and instinctively he followed her.

The Sitting-Room was empty, and the Duke knew without being told that Mr. Martin was not yet awake.

Without speaking Sarida moved quickly across to the opposite side of the room and opened a door.

"Lock yourself in," she whispered, "and do not make a sound!"

The Duke carrying his camera moved quickly into what he realised was Sarida's bedroom.

It was a small room, but beautifully furnished.

There were native rugs on the floor, a divan covered with an exquisitely embroidered Chinese shawl, and a number of satin cushions.

There were two very old Japanese prints on one wall, and there were several vases of flowers which filled the room with a Spring-like fragrance.

On what the Duke could see Sarida used as a dressing-table was a mirror which he felt sure she had found in some native shop.

It was hundreds of years old and carved with a skill and sensitivity which he knew could only have been found in Bali.

He thought the whole room portrayed what he might have expected would be Sarida's taste.

Then as he stood still against the door which he had locked, he heard horses drawing up outside the cottage and knew that their riders were dismounting.

Very cautiously he peeped through a small window veiled with white netting, which opened onto the front.

Now he could see who had arrived.

It was a large, heavily-built man wearing the uniform of a Dutch Colonel and with the somewhat bloated face of a man who drank too much.

The Duke was sure he was one of the Governors of the Javanese who treated them not only roughly, but as if they were dirt beneath his feet.

He looked in fact, judged by Western civilised standards, to be a thoroughly brutal type.

There were two soldiers with him, and the Duke knew they were an escort proclaiming his authority.

The Colonel opened the door of the cottage without knocking, which was in itself an insult.

As he walked into the room Sarida came ostensibly from her father's bedroom.

"*Goedemorgen*, Sarida!" the Dutchman said.

"Good morning, Colonel Van Keerck," Sarida replied. "I prefer to be addressed as '*Juffrouw*'."

The Colonel laughed.

"There is no need for such formality between us, and I have come to ask you Sarida, if you will dine with me tonight?"

There was a little pause before Sarida said:

"I am very honoured, Colonel, by your invitation. Unfortunately it is impossible for me to leave my father."

"He will be perfectly all right," the Colonel said. "If you want more servants to stay with him than he has already, I will send you some or else a couple of soldiers, if you prefer."

"I am sorry, *Mÿnheer*, but it is impossible."

"Nothing is impossible where you and I are concerned," the Colonel said. "I want to talk to you, I want to be with you alone, as I cannot be when you are here."

Sarida did not speak and after a moment he said:

"I will send a carriage for you at half-after-six."

"As I have already said, *Mÿnheer*, I cannot accept your invitation," Sarida replied.

The Colonel walked further into the room towards her.

"Now stop playing games! You know what I feel about you and you know what I can do for you."

He paused to look at her with leering, bloodshot eyes before he went on:

"I have found a house near to the Barracks where you will be very comfortable. You can bring your father there if you wish, but you must make it clear to him that he is in my house, and I can visit you whenever I please."

"I am not quite sure what you are suggesting," Sarida replied, "but I understand, *Mÿnheer* that you have a wife and several children in Holland. Surely you cannot have forgotten them?"

"Who has been talking?" the Colonel asked angrily. "And what has it got to do with anybody when we are here what is happening thousands of miles away in Europe?"

"It matters to me," Sarida retorted, "and therefore you must realise, Colonel, that I cannot accept your invitation, or your suggestion that we should share a house."

"Now you are being ridiculous!"

The Dutchman spoke in a different tone of voice.

"Can you not understand the difference I can make in your life? I am a rich man and I will give you jewellery, beautiful clothes, and a great deal more comfort than you have in this outlandish place!"

"My father and I are very happy here," Sarida said. "He has nearly finished his book and, as soon as he has done so, we are returning to England."

For a moment the Colonel was silent. Then he said:

"And you really think I would allow you to go? You forget, Sarida, that you must have Dutch permission to move about this country. I can make it impossible for you to board a ship or leave Java."

"I am a . . British citizen."

"You may find that difficult to prove," the Colonel said, and there was something sinister in the way he spoke.

He rose to his feet.

"My carriage will come for you at six-thirty, and if it comes back empty, you will find it impossible to go on living here. If I commandeer this cottage it then becomes mine rather than yours!"

Sarida drew in her breath. Then she said:

"I think you are threatening me, Colonel, and it is something I deeply resent! Kindly remember that my father is a sick man, and as I have already told you, it is impossible for me to leave him alone."

She spoke so positively that the Dutchman who had risen to his feet paused as he walked towards the door.

"Very well," he said, "if he is as sick as you say he is, I will give you time to get him better, but you will dine with me tomorrow night. Is that understood?"

He did not wait for Sarida's answer, but strode out of the cottage.

He left the door open and without moving she could see him mount his horse which was held by one of the soldiers.

When he had done so, he looked back at her, and the expression on his red face made her shudder.

Then he rode away, followed by his two soldiers, and the sound of their horses' hoofs gradually receded into the distance.

Only when they were nearly out of sight did the Duke unlock the bedroom door and open it.

Sarida, as he had somehow expected, was standing in the centre of the room staring out of the open doorway.

There was an expression on her face almost of despair.

The Duke walked to her side.

"How long has that swine been coming here and behaving in such an outrageous manner?" he asked.

"Unfortunately he saw me two weeks ago when I went into the city to do some shopping," Sarida answered. "I heard him asking the shop-keeper who I was, and because of course everything is known in Jogyakarta, the man told him."

"And he then came to visit you?"

"He . . arrived with his . . soldiers."

"And what happend?"

"He paid me . . compliments . . asked me to . . dine with him and I . . refused."

"And he will not give up? He has continued to frighten you ever since?" the Duke asked;

Sarida nodded. Then with a touch of horror in her voice she asked:

"What . . can I do? What can I . . say to him?"

"I would like to deal with him myself," the Duke said furiously.

"Oh . . no! You must . . not do . . that!" Sarida said quickly. "If you did he would be . . certain to . . find out that you have . . come from . . India!"

The Duke would have spoken but she went on:

"You could do . . nothing to . . prevent them from . . realising that you have been asked . . here for a . . special reason."

"Then they would find the Temple!" the Duke said beneath his breath.

"They would . . find it and . . rifle it," Sarida said despairingly.

"One thing is quite certain," the Duke said after what seemed a long silence, "you must never be alone with that man, however much he threatens you."

"I know . . that," Sarida said, "and I have . . excused myself half-a-dozen times . . already by saying that . . Papa is too ill to be left. Now . . as you heard . . his patience is becoming . . exhausted."

The Duke walked to the open door.

He stood looking out at the empty landscape, thinking it was shockingly bad luck, when she and her father had chosen such an isolated place in which to live, that somebody like Colonel Van Keerck should have found them.

He knew exactly the sort of licentious bully the man was.

The idea of him in close proximity to anything so delicate and beautiful as Sarida made him feel murderous.

He told himself this was something any decent man would feel about a young girl who was being pursued by a lecher of the worst type.

Then he knew that, because he and Sarida were joined to each other in a way he did not want to think about or acknowledge, his feelings were personal.

He turned round.

"Listen," he said to Sarida. "I will think of some way to prevent Van Keerck from pressing you to dine with him tomorrow night."

He thought as he spoke that perhaps he could ask the Sultan to invite the Dutchman to dinner.

Alternatively he might call himself on the Colonel and somehow make him at least postpone his invitation to Sarida.

He was not sure how it could be done, but he was absolutely convinced it was something he must do.

Then he was aware that Sarida was standing beside him and her hand was on his arm.

"Please," she pleaded, "do not become . . involved . . with this . . when there is . . something far more . . important at stake."

"If you mean the Temple," the Duke said, "I can only point out how long it has managed to survive, while at the moment the most pressing problem is yourself."

"I am not important," Sarida said.

The Duke looked at her incredulously.

He could not imagine any woman he had ever known in the past thinking that a Temple, however beautiful, however unique, was more important than her own safety.

And yet the way Sarida spoke told him she was completely sincere.

To her the Temple was far more important than her own feelings or the danger she was in as an attractive woman.

"Dammit all!" the Duke swore beneath his breath. "I will kill that swine rather than let him touch her!"

He did not question his feelings, he only knew they were there.

A little while later, the Duke knew it was time for him to return to the Palace.

The Colonel was by now so far ahead of him that he was most unlikely to overtake him on the road, nor would anybody in Jogyakarta know where he had been.

"I will develop the photographs," he told Sarida, "and if they are not good enough, we shall have to try again tomorrow."

He was just about to walk round to the back of the cottage to collect his horse when Sarida said:

"Perhaps I . . am being . . hysterical . . perhaps Colonel Van Keerck has . . upset me . . but . . could you come . . tonight?"

The words seemed to come from her lips reluctantly, and the Duke knew she was forcing herself to say them.

"You have a feeling something may happen?" he asked.

"I am . . trying to . . believe it is my . . imagination but it . . is there . . I know it is . . there!"

"In which case I will come to you as soon as I can get away from the Sultan."

"You will . . really come?"

She raised her eyes to his as she spoke, and he knew she had an almost childlike faith in him.

Then he told himself that she had no one else to whom she could turn, and he was, because he was English, the only person in whom she could confide.

"I will come!" he promised.

He turned to mount his horse.

"In the meantime, stay with your father, and if Van Keerck returns, do not see him alone."

"I would not have done so this morning . . if Papa had been awake," Sarida said. "But you will understand . . I do not wish to . . upset him . . and if Colonel Van Keerck threatens me . . I know Papa would be . . furious!"

"Quite justifiably so!" the Duke said. "The man is a disgrace to the uniform he wears. I will make it my business when I return to England to report him to the Dutch authorities!"

The Duke had spoken without thinking.

Now he realised that Sarida was looking at him in surprise.

She was thinking it was very unlikely that the Dutch would pay any attention to an ordinary Englishman in no position of authority.

The Duke knew he must retrieve his mistake, for he had spoken as himself.

"What is important," he said in a different tone of voice, "is that we should not think about anything so unpleasant. Go to the Temple, Sarida, and pray to the Lord Buddha, as you did yesterday. I know that he will protect you."

He saw Sarida's eyes light up.

"You understand!" she exclaimed. "You . . really understand!"

"Of course I do," the Duke said.

He knew as he spoke that it was the truth, and it was no use pretending any more. It was the truth.

As he rode back towards the Palace he admitted to himself that he was deeply involved with Sarida and was determined to protect her.

He also wanted to free her from a life which he felt inevitably, sooner or later, would end in disaster.

He knew what he was feeling was different from what he had ever felt for any woman before.

Always in the past, his feeling of possession had been entirely physical, and he had wanted them with a fiery desire which they all too readily reciprocated.

Sarida was different: so different that it was as inexpressible and extraordinary as was the likeness of her and himself to the reliefs of the Princess of Shailendra and King Rakai Pikatan.

"If I was sensible," a part of the Duke's brain was telling him, "I would go back to India and forget what is happening here in Java, or that I have ever met a girl called Sarida."

But his soul – a part of his make-up that he had not thought of for years – told him a very different tale.

He had found Sarida, and it was now impossible for him ever to lose her.

He could read her thoughts; he had known when she was praying that she had stepped into a mystical world in which he wished to follow her.

As a woman she was so lovely and at the same time so pure that he was afraid to touch her.

All the way as he rode back he was confronted by questions to which he could find no answers.

He knew that Sarida had to be saved from the Dutch just as he had to save the Temple from them and its treasures from the thieves.

But that was not the end.

When he took Sarida and her father back to England in his yacht, what would happen when they reached home?

Already she was in his thoughts, his mind, and if he was honest in his heart. He thought about her almost every moment of the day until he fell asleep.

Then she was in his dreams.

"I am not a young boy to fall in love so completely that the world is well lost for one woman!" he tried to tell himself angrily.

And yet as he entered the Palace and moved to the pavilion where he knew he would find the Sultan, he felt that Sarida was beside him.

There was no escape for either of them.

Chapter Six

In the afternoon there was a torrential downpour of rain, as happened almost every day during the rainy season.

It did not last for long, but the streets were soon awash, the paddy-fields flooded and everybody sought shelter.

The Duke, fortunately had not left the Palace, and went with Dawson to the dark-room.

They finished developing and printing all the photographs he had taken since he arrived in Jogyakarta.

When he showed his pictures of the Concubines to the Sultan he was delighted.

It was something he had never had before and never expected to have.

The Duke realised he could not have given him a more acceptable present, whatever he brought him.

Later, when the rain had stopped, he took some more photographs of the Palace and thought they would be interesting to show to George Curzon.

He supposed that he should arrange to go to Borobudur, but it was a journey which would take the whole day.

For the moment he had no wish to leave Sarida.

He found himself worrying over her problem with Colonel Van Keerck and how she could avoid the man.

There was one obvious answer to this, but he refused even to think of it and told himself he was being ridiculous.

And yet, every hour of the day he found himself wondering how he could leave Jogyakarta and Sarida behind.

He knew she would be eventually helpless against the Dutch bully, especially if her father was too ill for them to move away or return home.

The hours passed slowly, until at last it was time for him to dine with the Sultan.

In any other circumstances, he thought afterwards, he would have enjoyed the meal he had had with such an intelligent man.

There was a great deal he could learn from him about the country.

But whatever they were discussing, he felt as if he could see nothing but Sarida's eyes pleading with him.

He could hear the little tremor of fear in her voice when she had spoken of the Dutch Colonel.

At last dinner was finished.

The Sultan said goodnight and the Duke now free, walked hastily to where he knew Hadji would be waiting for him.

It was Hadji who ordered a horse when he needed it, knowing it was a mistake for the request to go through the servants.

They would think it strange that he rode so early in the morning, and so late at night.

He had sent a message to Hadji to say he wished to see him, and the Javanese taking one look at him said perceptively:

"Do you think that something is going to happen tonight?"

"Sarida thinks so," the Duke answered.

"Are you going alone? I could find someone I can trust to go with you."

The Duke shook his head.

"It would be dangerous for anyone to know about it. Besides, Sarida may be wrong. She has no particular grounds for thinking that tonight is important."

"Sarida is very close to the gods," Hadji said softly, "and they speak with tongues we cannot hear."

The Duke did not answer.

Only when he had ridden away from the Palace did he tell himself angrily that he refused to listen to all this spooky nonsense!

The sooner he returned to Europe, the better.

Then he knew that was not what he really thought, and he was glad that he had his revolver with him.

'I am ready for a combat with reality,' he thought as he rode on, 'not with delusions or fantasies that have nothing to do with fact!'

Darkness had fallen and the stars were coming out like diamonds in the sky and there was a full moon.

The road was still wet with the rain, so he did not ride very fast.

It was impossible not to be thrilled by the beauty of the palm trees against the stars, the villages with a light in the windows of the bamboo cottages.

When he was out of the City he looked to where in the distance there was the volcanic mountain which so many centuries ago had erupted over Borobudur.

In the daytime he had seen it smoking against the sky, but now there was only the moonlight turning the padi-fields to silver.

At last he turned off the road to ride over the rough track which would eventually lead him to Plaosan.

Now he was nearer to Sarida and he found himself asking again the same question. What should he do about her?

He knew he could not offer her what Colonel Van Keerck had offered.

It would be insulting and degrading not only because she was obviously a Lady by birth, but also because she was pure and innocent.

Yet what else could he do?

It was impossible for him as a Duke to marry somebody of no consequence in England who had lived in the same County as himself without his being aware of it.

The Duke was very conscious of the importance of his family.

All down the centuries his ancestors had allied themselves with the great families of England.

"Blue blood must go with blue blood," he had heard his father say when he was only a small boy.

When he grew older it had been drilled into him by everybody from his grandparents to his distant cousins that the woman who became his wife must be worthy of the position.

Her blood and her antecedents must match his.

He knew that some of his more perceptive relatives had been aware of Lady Charlotte's true nature and the gossips had chattered about her promiscuous behaviour.

Nevertheless they considered her a suitable bride for the Duke of Inglebury.

He could imagine all too easily the horror with which they would receive his marriage to an unknown girl called Miss Martin, however beautiful she might be.

"What am I to do?" the Duke asked. "What the devil am I to do?"

It was then, as he rode towards the cottage which he could see in the distance, that he became aware that ahead of him, nearing the wood, there was something moving.

A little further on he saw that it was not animals, as he had at first thought, but three men, and they were pulling something along the ground.

He could not imagine what it could be.

But he guided his horse off the road and onto the soft wet grass which sloped down to the water which had been much increased by the rain.

He made no sound as he rode on, but as the ground was

so soft his horse moved at a slower pace than before.

As the Duke saw the men disappearing into the wood, he knew that they must be the thieves.

It was then with a jolt he remembered that as he had turned off the road he had noticed almost without realising it a cart drawn by two horses standing near some palm trees.

As there was no one with it he had not given it a second thought, but now he thought there was an obvious reason for it being there.

By the time he reached the trees which obscured the Temple the men had disappeared, but he knew where they had gone.

Quickly he dismounted, drew the revolver from his pocket, and walked cautiously through the trees.

When he was nearly there, the moonlight coming through the branches of the trees overhead showed him what lay ahead.

Two of the men who had been dragging something after them were spreading it in front of the Temple towards which the third man was walking.

The Duke could see him quite clearly for the moonlight was on his face.

He was thick-set, short of stature, and nearing middle-age.

The Duke thought, although he was not sure, that he was not entirely Javanese.

He held in his hand a *kris*, the long sharp-pointed carved knife that every native carried.

The Duke's fingers tightened on his revolver.

As the man reached the bottom of the stones which lay beneath the entrance to the Temple, he stepped forward to challenge him.

As he did so from the opening of the Temple Sarida appeared.

She rose to her feet as she came through the falling vines, then stood looking in horror at the man below her.

If she was surprised to see him, he was also surprised to see her.

Neither he nor the Duke moved.

Then as Sarida threw out her arms as if to protect what lay behind her, the thief moved forward.

He raised the *kris* high above his head as if he intended to thrust it into her body.

Without pausing, without even thinking what he must do except that he must save Sarida, the Duke lifted his revolver and fired.

Aimed by a crack shot the bullet entered the man's head at the side of his temple, and he fell to the ground as if pole-axed.

The explosion of the shot echoed violently round the wood.

The other two men, who were still concerning themselves with what they had been pulling, turned and ran.

They hurled themselves through the trees, twisting and turning desperately to get away.

Then once clear of the wood they were running as fast as they could, back to where their cart was waiting.

The Duke walked forward.

He stepped over the dead man lying on the ground.

Then he put out his arms and lifted Sarida, who seemed frozen into immobility, down from the Temple.

He held her close against him and she hid her face on his shoulder.

"It is all right, my darling," he said quietly. "He is dead, and no longer a threat to you or the Temple."

She was not crying, but he could feel her whole body trembling against him.

He knew then that he loved her as he had never loved any woman before.

If he lost her, he would lose something so precious that

he would feel crippled for the rest of his life.

He held her closely, his lips on her hair, thanking God he had been in time.

They stood together in silence.

There was no sound, not even the retreating footsteps of the other two thieves could be heard.

Gently the Duke lifted Sarida over the prostrate body which now lay directly behind them.

"Go back to the cottage," he said, "I will join you in a few minutes."

She made a little murmur.

He took his arms from her and turning her round in the direction of the cottage, waited until she had moved slowly away.

He watched her until he realised she was obeying him like a puppet and would reach the cottage in safety.

Then he picked up the body of the man he had shot.

He carried it a few yards to where lying on the ground was what he realised was a rough slide made of some heavy material.

The men had dragged it from the cart so that they could put the statues they intended to steal on it, and no one in the cottage would hear them pass.

It was a clever idea, and having thrown the man he had shot down onto it, the Duke pulled it through the trees out onto some hard ground, and then down to the water.

Lifting the dead man up in his arms, the Duke carried him over the sloping grass and threw him as far as he could, face downwards, into what was now a swollen lake.

As the man's body fell he watched anxiously in case the lake was more shallow than he thought it to be.

But the body disappeared completely, and the Duke knew that it would be a long time, perhaps months, before the water dried away and by that time he would be unrecognisable.

He picked up the slide and threw that too but into a

different place.

For a few seconds it floated, then gradually the water closed over it and disappeared.

The Duke walked back to the cottage.

His horse was foraging outside the wood but he did not trouble himself with it.

Instead he walked through the garden to where the door stood open and Sarida was standing outside.

She was waiting for him and her eyes seemed to fill her whole face as she looked at him enquiringly.

He walked towards her, took her in his arms, and without speaking his lips came down on hers.

For a moment she stiffened in sheer surprise.

Then as his mouth held her captive he felt her surrender herself.

Her lips were soft and sweet and her whole body seemed to melt into his so that they were one person, as she knew they had been long ago.

His kiss became more demanding, more possessive and she was not frightened, but responded to him both with her body and with her soul.

As he kissed her and went on kissing her, he knew that never in his life had any other woman evoked in him what he was feeling now.

It was not the fiery passion of desire that he had known with Charlotte and so many other women like her.

It was something so spiritual that he felt a rapture and an ecstasy that he had never believed possible.

He knew that Sarida was feeling the same, and that their kiss had carried them into the world of the Divine which she entered in her prayers.

Only when they both touched something so mystic and wonderful that came from the gods did the Duke raise his head.

As he looked at Sarida in the light of the oil-lamp he

thought it would be impossible for any woman to be more beautiful and still be human.

For a moment they just looked at each other.

Then, as if Sarida broke under the strain, she said in a rapt little voice:

"I . . I love . . you . . I love . . you!"

"As I love you!" the Duke said. "How can you make me feel like this? How is it possible, after I have been looking for you all my life, that I should find you in such a strange way?"

She did not answer, but only lifted her lips towards him as if that was the only way she could express what she was feeling.

The Duke in a voice he hardly recognised as his own said:

"I love you! God, how I love you! How soon will you marry me, my darling?"

Then without waiting for her reply he was kissing her again.

Kissing her until they both felt they had touched the sky and the stars were shining within them.

It might have been a long time or even a century later that Sarida asked a little hesitatingly:

'W.what have you . . done?"

"I have thrown him into the water," the Duke answered.

He thought as he spoke that his voice sounded unsteady.

"He will never again be able to thieve from the Temple, and it is safe."

"Are you . . certain . . quite certain the other men . . will not . . come back?"

"They will be far too frightened to do so."

Sarida gave a deep sigh, then the Duke said:

"How could you have done anything so dangerous as to go there when you promised me to take care of yourself?"

"I . . I did not . . mean to disobey you," Sarida said in a low voice, "but . . Papa is d.dead . . and I wanted to pray

111

for him to the . . Lord Buddha."

"Your father is dead?" the Duke repeated as if his brain found it hard to understand what she had said.

"He finished his book," Sarida said, "and I am sure it was the way he would have wanted to leave us."

The Duke knew she was not crying because she believed that her father was not really dead, but had gone to a place where sooner or later he would find another body.

He did not know how he knew this, but it was as if he could read Sarida's thoughts.

Then as if she read his, she said:

"Now I . . must go.h.home."

It was as if she was speaking to herself, and he knew again perceptively that she was not imposing herself on him, but merely stating a fact.

"I asked you to marry me, my precious," he said.

She looked up at him searchingly before she asked:

"Are you . . sure that is . . what you want?"

"More than I have ever wanted anything in my whole life! But you are aware that the first thing we have to do is to escape from this country?"

As if she suddenly remembered Colonel Van Keerck, Sarida stiffened and the Duke said:

"Do not be afraid. We will get away."

Even as he spoke there was the sound of a footstep outside and they were suddenly still.

The Duke looking at Sarida saw an expression of fear in her eyes.

Then through the open door came Hadji.

"May I come in?" he asked.

"Hadji!" the Duke exclaimed with relief.

The older man came into the Sitting-Room.

"I followed you," he said to the Duke, "just in case you should run into danger."

"I did run into danger," the Duke replied. "But I have

killed the leader of the thieves, and the other two have run away."

"I saw that," Hadji said, "and they will not come back."

The Duke waited for an explanation, and Hadji went on:

"I realised what must have happened, and as they climbed into their cart I cursed them in a manner which will frighten them for the rest of their lives!"

Sarida gave a little cry.

"That was clever of you! I expect they were only the . . servants of their leader who is now . . dead."

"You have done our country a great service," Hadji said to the Duke.

"I have accomplished what the Viceroy asked me to do," the Duke replied. "Now, Hadji, you have to help me to get Sarida away without there being any trouble with Van Keerck."

Hadji nodded as if he was aware of that, and the Duke said:

"It would be easier if we were married. Is there a Christian priest of any sort in Jogyakarta?"

Hadji thought for a moment, then he shook his head.

The Duke looked at Sarida with a worried expression on his face.

He recalled that in the Moslem faith there was no priesthood.

Moreover he knew that the Officers of the Mosques, or Imams, who performed marriages would insist on one of them being Moslem before they were joined.

He felt Sarida move a little closer to him as if she was afraid they might be separated.

Then before he could reassure her that whatever the difficulties they would get away together, Hadji said:

"My brother could marry you."

He spoke a little tentatively, as if he was afraid of what they would think of such an idea.

"Your brother?" the Duke asked.

"He is a Priest in Badung in South Bali, where there are no Dutch."

He knew that the two people facing him were listening intently as he went on:

"He has come here secretly because he has to bless the paddy-fields. Our people will not work unless they are sure that Devi Sri, the Goddess of rice, is helping them."

The Duke was well aware how the Dutch would 'pooh-pooh' such an idea.

But to the Javanese the spirits of their gods had to be placated and revered.

Spirits dominated the Javanese world, and watched over the welfare of each community, its land and its people.

He was aware of this from what he had read on his way to Java.

He knew that to Sarida it was not only what she knew, but what she believed.

She raised her eyes to his and he smiled at her before he said to Hadji:

"We would be very honoured if your brother would marry us, and where else but in the Temple which has brought us together?"

Sarida gave a little cry of happiness and Hadji said:

"I will, Sir, arrange it for early tomorrow morning, so that no-one will know what is happening. Afterwards I know that the Sultan will help you in every way you require."

"Thank you," the Duke said.

It was then that Sarida moved away from his arms and taking Hadji by the hand she said in his own language:

"Papa, who was your friend, has left us."

Hadji stiffened then he asked:

"He had completed his task?"

"He finished his book," Sarida answered.

Hadji walked across the room and opened the door of Mr. Martin's bedroom and went inside.

Sarida did not go with him, but turned back to the Duke.

"Is it . . true . . really true that I am to be . . your wife?" she asked.

"I have discovered that I cannot live without you," the Duke answered.

"Then . . we shall be . . together . . as we were . . before."

He knew exactly what she was saying and he looked at her very tenderly. Then said:

"We will be married in the Temple we built so long ago, and perhaps, now that we have found each other, there will be other Temples that will help and sustain people, as ours has done."

For the first time there were tears in Sarida's eyes.

"How could you . . say anything so . . wonderful?" she asked. "How could . . you . . understand as I thought no man would be . . able to do."

"It is something I never expected," the Duke said honestly, "but I think love has changed me."

"I do not want you changed . . I want you just as you are . . kind, understanding and . . very strong and protective."

"That is what I intend to be," the Duke replied, "but you know as well as I do that we must get out of this land without there being a fuss. I have no doubt that Van Keerck will try to prevent you from leaving."

Sarida shuddered and he put his arms around her.

"Leave everything to me," he said. "I am just worrying about one thing."

"What is that?"

"How we shall bury your father."

There was silence for a moment.

Then Sarida hid her face against him as she was half-afraid to say what she was thinking."

"What is it, my darling?" the Duke asked. "You know I will do anything you want me to do, but we must be very careful.."

"I am . . aware of that," Sarida said, "but I know the way . . Papa would like to be buried . . especially here . . in a country which he loved."

"How is that?" the Duke asked after a moment.

He was thinking as he asked the question that the easiest way would be to bury Mr. Martin in the wood beside the Temple.

Yet he was afraid that Sarida would not want to leave her father in some unmarked grave in a strange land where she could never visit it.

Then, after a little pause, Sarida said:

"I know that Papa would like more than . . anything else to have a Hindu burial . . and it is something which would be . . very easy to do."

The Duke stared at her in astonishment. Then he asked:

"What do you mean by that?"

"I mean," Sarida said bravely, "that his funeral pyre should be the cottage! He believed it would be . . unsafe to leave it standing in case anyone who . . lived in it should perhaps discover and explore the Temple."

"And you think your father should be burned in it?"

"I . . I know that is what he would . . want in the circumstances . . and what does it matter what happens to his body? His spirit is with God!"

The Duke took her hand and raised it to his lips.

"You are very brave, my lovely one," he said, "and I know that that is the right thing for us to do."

"We will be . . married," Sarida whispered, "and I know that Papa will be . . watching us . . and afterwards . . when the cottage has burned to the ground . . nobody will be . . interested."

As she finished speaking Hadji came back into the room.

The Duke told him briefly what they intended to do and the old man said:

"That is wise – very wise! But now, Sir, I think you should go back to the Palace."

The Duke frowned.

"I intended to stay here to protect Sarida."

"I will do that," Hadji said. "I have many prayers to say for the man who was so brilliant and learned, who has written of our religions, and knew so much about them. In his next life, he will be a Bodhisattva."

The Duke knew that a Bodhisattva had only one more life to live before he reached Nirvana, and he was aware that no-one could be paid a greater compliment.

He saw how much Sarida appreciated this, and she said:

"Thank you, and I know Papa would be very . . proud of what . . you have . . said about him."

Hadji bowed. Then he said to the Duke;

"When you reach the Palace ask to see the Sultan who will not be asleep. Ask him to lend you horses and a carriage to carry you to the sea."

"I am sure he will do that," the Duke said. "And what about your brother?"

"I will stay here until the night is almost past," Hadji replied, "then return to collect him. He is at my house and there will be no difficulty."

"I can only thank you from the bottom of my heart," the Duke said.

Hadji bowed.

He then left the Sitting-Room to return once more to Mr. Martin's bedroom.

The Duke put his arms around Sarida.

"We will do what Hadji suggests, my darling."

"Are you . . quite sure it is . . what you want?" Sarida asked.

"I want you to be my wife," the Duke said, "and though it will be a strange marriage, we shall both believe we are married in the sight of God."

He pulled her a little closer before he said:

"We shall of course have to conform to the world in which we will live. We can be married by the Captain of my yacht once we are at sea, which is entirely legal, and again when we reach Calcutta, in the Viceroy's Private Chapel."

"Is that where we are going?" Sarida enquired.

"That is where we will go first," the Duke said, "because I shall have to report to Lord Curzon how I have carried out his wishes, and that I believe the Temple is now safe for perhaps another century."

"You have been so wonderful!" Sarida whispered.

Then the Duke was kissing her, kissing her until the room whirled around them and once again they were swept into the sky and were one with the gods.

It was with the greatest difficulty that the Duke took his arms from Sarida.

"I had better go," he said at last, "or the Sultan will have gone to bed."

"Then go quickly," Sarida said, "and remember that . . tomorrow evening . . the . . Colonel is sending a . . c.carriage for me."

"He will be both surprised and disappointed!" the Duke remarked.

He kissed her again and went towards the door.

Outside he saw that not only was Hadji's horse tied to a fence, but so was his own.

He mounted, aware that Sarida was watching him from the door, and he waved to her before he rode off.

Then as he travelled as swiftly as he could towards the Palace he was thinking how extraordinary everything had been.

He had found the thief who had taken away the Buddha and killed him.

At the same time, he had found that he would not live without Sarida.

Whatever his family or anybody else might say, she was the only thing that mattered to him.

He had come to Java because George Curzon had asked him to, and also because he wanted to escape from Lady Charlotte.

Now he would be leaving it not only having accomplished his mission, but also having discovered both love and his soul.

He knew now that Sarida had opened his mind, shown him new horizons that he had never envisaged before.

The Temple, with his own relief on the walls of it, had changed his whole thinking about the After Life, and the Power that directs all human beings.

He knew that his whole attitude towards living would be different in the future.

There was so much to learn, so much to understand, so much to achieve that had never been there before.

To do all this he needed Sarida, and tomorrow she would be his.

Once again he was saying to the Spirits that were all around him and which he could feel in his mind, his heart and his soul:

"Thank You! Thank You!"

Chapter Seven

When Hadji called for him early the next morning, the Duke found it hard for a moment to remember it was his Wedding Day.

He had talked with the Sultan the night before, who had told him over and over again how grateful he was that the thief who had stolen the Buddha was dead.

He was quite sure that his accomplices would not go back.

"Perhaps now that the whole country is alert to the value of Borobudur," His Royal Highness said, "the Dutch will pay more attention to our pleas that the Temples they have already found are not rifled."

"I think that with the support of the Viceroy the world outside Java will also alert the Dutch to their responsibilities," the Duke added.

He knew when he left the Sultan he had done the country a service that would never be forgotten.

The Sultan was only too happy to provide him with the carriage and horses he needed to take Sarida to the sea.

The Duke had fallen asleep thinking of his bride-to-be and telling himself once again that he was the luckiest man in the world.

He was sensible enough to be aware that there would be many difficulties ahead when they reached England, especially from his relatives.

He knew however, that if he lost Sarida, if she were not

his wife, he would be like a man crippled.

"I love her," he said to the stars before he got into bed, "and I know she loves me!"

Dawson had packed their luggage and it was already in the carriage that was waiting for them at the Palace gate.

There was no-one to bid him farewell.

It would have been a mistake for the *Aides-de-Camp* to know he was leaving so precipitately and he had no wish for anybody to be curious.

There was therefore only a Javanese driver on the box of the carriage, and Dawson jumped up beside him.

The Duke sat inside finding it was unexpectedly well-sprung.

It was drawn by two well bred and spirited horses by which he knew he could travel a great deal more swiftly than he had by rickshaw to Jogyakarta.

He had already instructed Dawson what to do.

The carriage came to a halt some way from the cottage, in fact, almost opposite the place where he had thrown the thief into the water.

There had been a heavy rainstorm during the night and the Duke saw with satisfaction that the water was even higher than it had been the previous day.

Leaving the carriage, he walked the short distance that remained to the cottage.

He was aware as he did so, that the last stars were fading in the sky, and there was the first faint glow of dawn in the East.

There was also, he was aware, that strange hush which always comes before the dawn and makes one feel that the drama of a new day is about to unfold.

The Duke knew that was what it would be for him.

He felt a surge of excitement seep through him, knowing that in a few seconds he would be with Sarida.

She was waiting for him just inside the cottage.

As he walked in through the open door, he realised he was seeing her for the first time in European dress.

Always before she had worn a sarong.

Now she was wearing a white gown that was very plain, but clung to her figure and made her look all the more like her relief on the Temple.

There was a short veil over her fair hair and a wreath of white flowers which had been picked from the garden to hold it in place.

She looked so lovely that for a moment the Duke could only stand and stare at her.

He felt she could not be real; she could only be one of the Spirits they were both vividly aware were near them.

As their eyes met, he knew they were already so close to each other, so much a part of one another, that not all the ceremonies there were could make them any closer.

Then in a voice it was hard to hear, Sarida said:

"Y.you have . . come!"

"To make you my wife, my darling," the Duke answered.

He drew nearer to her and as she put out her hands he took them and raised them to his lips.

"I love you!" he said. "Later I will be able to tell you how much!"

She gave him a sweet smile, before she said softly:

"The Priest . . is waiting."

The Duke held her hand in his and they walked out through the cottage door across the garden into the wood.

By the time they had reached the trees, the first ray of sunshine had flashed over the horizon.

As the gold of it flickered through the branches, the Duke thought it was a symbol of their happiness.

When they reached the Temple he saw that the vines in front of the entrance had been pulled to one side.

When they had climbed over the stones which should

have been the steps there was no need for them to go down on their knees.

They stood for a moment in the light, then entered through the doorway.

Inside the Duke saw that the place where the Buddha had sat was filled with candles.

There were also a number of them on each side of the Bodhisattvas.

The whole chamber was dazzling with light and fragrant with incense from the joss-sticks.

Then he was aware that the Priest was kneeling down before a small table, which he knew was a shrine.

He was wearing a dark green *sarong* and a white *baju* or cap of his Office.

Before him on the table was a brass bell, Holy Water in a bowl, and some flowers.

The Duke was aware that he and Sarida must kneel on their heels on Eastern rugs she had brought from the cottage.

As they did so Hadji, who had been standing at the side of the chamber, handed the Duke an offering of fruit, laid out on a palm leaf.

He understood he was to hand it to the Priest.

It was dedicated by the Priest touching his bell, praying silently, breaking off a piece from the leaf and touching it with drops of Holy Water.

After that he sat with his eyes closed praying and making rhythmic gestures with his hand over the fruit towards the bride and bridegroom.

It was then, as Sarida prayed that she might make the Duke happy, he was aware that there were Spirits in the chamber, watching over them and blessing them.

He could feel them so strongly that it was almost as if he could see them, and the whole Temple seemed to come alive.

At last, the Priest rose and, taking up his bowl of Holy Water, sprinkled drops of it onto Sarida's head, then on the Duke's.

He gave Sarida a square of palm leaf and the Duke was handed a jewel-handled *kris*.

He pierced the leaf with it and knew this had a sacred meaning.

Finally the Priest handed both the bride and bridegroom eggs which were a symbol of fertility.

As he passed from one to the other the Priest rang his brass bell, then raised his arms to the gods above and called for their blessing.

Sarida looked at the Duke and he knew from the expression in her eyes that she was praying that she would give him sons as strong and handsome and protective as he was.

When she knew he understood her prayer, the colour rose in her cheeks and her eye-lids dropped because she was shy.

He knew then that she was pure in her mind and her body, as he had always wanted his wife to be.

He knew too that she was very innocent.

He vowed that he would keep her safe from everything crude, evil and ugly, so that the spiritual bond between them would never be soiled or damaged.

As these thoughts passed through his mind, he felt his love rise like a flame within him.

What he felt seemed to mingle with the light of the candles and the Spirits that encompassed them and the glory of Heaven itself.

It was a feeling of ecstasy that he could not put into words.

And yet he knew it came from the Divine and he was richly privileged to feel it.

He was aware that Sarida was experiencing the same feelings, and her face was transfigured by an ecstasy which came from her soul and was part of the gods.

Finally they both rose to their feet, and the Priest followed by Hadji left the Temple.

The Duke looked down at Sarida and said very gently:

"Now you are my wife!"

"I pray that I . . may never . . fail you," she whispered.

For a moment they stood looking into each other's eyes.

Then the Duke led Sarida out into the sunshine and they followed the Priest and Hadji through the trees and on towards the cottage.

When they reached it the Duke saw what he had not noticed when he arrived, that Sarida's luggage was waiting at the end of the garden.

There were also several other things beside it.

He recognised the carved mirror from her dressing-table, and two rolled up bundles which he knew were the Japanese prints.

He guessed Sarida had given them as presents to Hadji.

They walked through the flowers to where a little distance from the cottage on a piece of raised ground there lay another rug.

Sarida sat down on her heels as they had sat in the Temple, and the Duke did the same.

Now the Priest was standing in front of the cottage praying and again raising his arms to the gods.

Then, so quickly that the Duke knew Hadji must have prepared it carefully beforehand, flames began to rise from the thatched roof of the cottage.

Within a few minutes the whole building was alight.

Then there was only the crackling of the wood and the Priest's voice as he prayed for the soul of Sarida's father.

As he did so the sun, warm and golden, enveloped them and seemed to mingle with the leaping flames to make it impossible to see clearly.

But the Duke knew that Sarida believed her father's soul

was being carried by the Divine Light into another world.

When the flames were at their highest and the whole cottage was ablaze, Hadji came to the Duke and touched him on the shoulder.

He rose to his feet and moved a little to one side.

Sarida, whose eyes were closed, was not aware of it and Hadji said in a low voice:

"You should leave now, everything is arranged."

The Duke drew a large sum of money he had brought with him from his pocket as an offering to the Priest.

As he took it, Hadji said:

"The carriage will take you to my house in the country where I thought you should stay the night."

The Duke looked surprised, but he did not speak, and Hadji went on:

"I know you have to signal for your yacht to come into the bay, but it is best you board it early in the morning before there are many people about."

The Duke knew this was wise, and Hadji continued:

"You will be comfortable in my house, and I hope very happy there."

"I do not know how I can thank you . . . " the Duke began.

Hadji held up his hand to prevent him from saying anything more.

"We people of Java are too deeply in your debt, Sir, to be able to express our feelings in words."

The Duke understood, and he said:

"I too am more grateful than I can say for the manner by which you arranged our marriage, as well as Mr. Martin's Funeral."

Hadji bowed reverently.

The Duke was aware that while they had been talking, the carriage had moved nearer to the cottage and was now just outside the garden.

126

He therefore wasted no more time, and going back to Sarida bent down to lift her to her feet.

"It is time for us to leave, my darling," he said quietly.

He was aware as he spoke that she was concentrating so intently on her father that it took a moment for her to comprehend what he had said.

Then she gave him a little smile and he admired her bravery and her unshakeable belief that her father was still alive in another world.

He knew she felt her father was near her, even though she could no longer see him.

The Duke put his arm around her and drew her out of the garden towards the carriage.

As they stepped inside it, Hadji said very sincerely:

"The gods go with you."

Before they could reply he had shut the door of the carriage and the horses moved off.

It was still so early that there were few people about in the streets of Jogyakarta and therefore no one of importance to look at them with curiosity.

Only when they were well away from the City and out into the countryside did the Duke stop the carriage to take over the reins.

Sarida was beside him while the coachman and Dawson sat inside.

As they drove on she said with a little laugh:

"I knew this was what you wanted to do!"

"They are not as fine as the horses I have at home," the Duke said, "but I am sure I shall get us more quickly to our destination than the coachman would have done."

Sarida laughed.

"That is a challenge, and I believe it is quite a long way."

"This is a strange way to start our honeymoon," the Duke said, "but just as our marriage was different and strange, so this is something we will always remember."

"To me it was wonderful," Sarida said, "and the gods were there with us."

It was what the Duke had felt so vividly that he knew he would never question the truth of it.

They drove for some way in silence.

Then Sarida put her hand on the Duke's hand as if to make sure he was there and asked a little nervously:

"Have we really escaped? You do not think Colonel Van Keerck will follow us?"

The Duke knew that to her it was a very real fear.

"He will not know until tonight," he replied, "when the carriage returns without you, that the cottage is burnt to the ground and you are not there."

He felt Sarida give a little quiver and went on:

"By the time he realises you have gone and has made enquiries, it will be far too late for him to make the journey we are making now."

He knew that Sarida relaxed and he said:

"Tomorrow at dawn we leave Java and the Dutch behind. They are the past – England and home is the future."

The radiance was back in Sarida's eyes.

It took only five hours for the Duke to reach Hadji's house.

It was built high above the road and the water-filled padi-fields.

In the distance it looked like a long white strip surrounded by palm trees.

When they reached it the Duke saw it was a very well built one-storey house with a tiled roof and a long verandah.

He had thought that whatever it was like it would be preferable to the cottages in which he had slept on his way to Jogyakarta.

And any building would be a welcome protection from

128

the sun which had grown very hot as the day progressed.

The house had large windows, many of them without any glass, wooden floors covered by native rugs, and because it was high on a hill there was a faint breeze to cool the air.

As soon as they arrived the Duke was aware that Hadji must have sent a messenger the night before to inform the servants of their arrival.

There were fruit-drinks waiting for them, and a light meal of fresh fish and Javanese dishes which they both enjoyed.

When the meal was over the Duke said:

"I know, my darling, you must have slept very little last night, and as all sensible people in the East take a *siesta* at this time so I suggest that is what we do now.'

Sarida smiled at him and moved towards the room which she had been shown when she arrived.

The Duke went to another room to find Dawson had unpacked his things and also provided him with a cold bath.

When he had dried himself he put on a thin linen robe which he had brought with him in the yacht, and opened the door into Sarida's bedroom.

It was, he saw, a beautiful room, and the sun-blinds were lowered outside so that it was dim and cool.

The bed was a large mattress raised a few inches from the floor with a headboard of coloured carving.

It was piled with silk cushions, and lying amongst them, looking like a Princess in a Fairy-Tale, Sarida was fast asleep.

Her fair hair was flowing over her shoulders, and the Duke thought it was longer and more beautiful even than he had imagined.

He stood looking down at her, and because she was so exquisite he felt the blood throbbing in his temples.

He wanted almost unbearably to take her in his arms and kiss her into wakefulness.

Then he knew because he loved her he must be unselfish and let her sleep.

She had been through two very emotional experiences today – her wedding, which he knew had aroused a spiritual ecstasy within her, and her father's Funeral.

It was magnificent and majestic in its way, but it was still painful for Sarida to have lost him physically.

Very quietly the Duke went to the other side of the bed and lowered himself gently onto it.

He covered himself with the same sheet that Sarida had pulled up to her waist, without waking her.

He was aware as he did so that a faint, fresh fragrance emanated from her like that of the flowers in the garden.

He knew too that he had been right in thinking that her body was like that of a Greek Goddess.

He could see the soft curves of her breasts beneath the thin material of her nightgown.

No woman, he told himself, could be more lovely or perfect.

Yet he loved her for many other reasons besides her beauty.

She had told him while they were driving here that she had given Hadji the carved mirror that he had admired in her bedroom and the Japanese prints.

She had also paid the servants generously and given them everything that was in the kitchen, besides a number of sheets and towels which she knew they would appreciate.

She had done that last night before she went to bed, then sent them home to their own house in the nearby village.

The Duke could not help wondering how many of all the other women he had known, would have been so considerate.

He was thinking of Sarida and how much he loved her when without intending to do so, he fell asleep.

*

When the Duke awoke, he was aware that they must both have slept for several hours.

The sun was not as hot as it had been, and the shadows were beginning to lengthen beneath the palm-trees.

There was a faint breeze stirring the branches overhead and he thought there was a taste of salt in the air, which meant they were not very far from the sea.

Tomorrow they would be aboard the *Sea Hawk* and safe from everything that had frightened Sarida.

He turned over and raised himself on his elbow to look down at her.

She was still asleep, and there was a faint smile on her lips. which he knew was one of happiness.

Then as he told himself he could wait no longer to kiss her, her eyes opened and she said in a soft little voice:

"You are . . real?"

It was what she had said to him the first time he had seen her and he answered:

"I am real, my darling, and so are you."

His lips came down on hers and he kissed her at first gently, then more possessively.

"I . . I love you . . and I was . . dreaming of you," Sarida said.

"Now there is no need to dream," the Duke answered, "because we are together. You are mine, Sarida, my wife and I adore you!"

Then he was kissing her with long, demanding kisses which grew more passionate.

He kissed her eyes, her little straight nose, then as her lips waited for his, the softness of her neck.

It gave her strange sensations that she had never known, and he felt her body quivering against his.

Now he knew a little flame was rising within her to meet the fire that threatened to consume him.

He felt the heat of it seeping through her body.

At the same time, he knew because she was so young, so innocent and so pure, that he must be very controlled, so as not to frighten her.

He raised his head.

"I love you," he said, "God, how much I love you, but I would not do anything, my precious darling, that you would not want me to."

"I . . I want you to . . love me," she whispered. "I am . . your wife . . we are one person."

Just for a moment the Duke hesitated, then she said:

"I love you . . I love you with . . all of me! I want to . . belong to you . . completely. Love me . . please . . love me . . . !"

There was a rapt note in her voice and it made the Duke feel as if she lifted him into the Spirit World which was so close to her.

There was nothing evil or ugly to spoil the beauty and the wonder of it.

"You are mine – mine," he said in his heart.

Then as he made Sarida his he knew they touched the very peak of Divine ecstasy and they were one with the gods.

A long time later when the sun was sinking in a blaze of glory Sarida kissed the Duke's naked shoulder and said:

"You have . . heard it before . . but I love you!"

"I can never hear it too often."

He pulled her a little closer before he asked:

"I have not hurt or frightened you, my lovely one?"

"How could I be . . frightened of you . . when you have . . saved and . . protected me?"

"It is something I will do all my life," the Duke vowed.

"All our . . *lives*," Sarida corrected softly.

He moved his lips over her hair before he asked:

"How can you be so perfect in every way and so different

from any woman I have ever known?"

"I . . am really . . different?" Sarida asked.

"Very, very different," the Duke said, "and I not only adore you for your beauty, but I worship your purity and because, Heart of my Heart, you are good."

"I will try always to be good for you," Sarida answered.

Then she hid her face against his neck and whispered:

"And . . for . . our . . children."

The Duke's lips were on her hair.

He knew this was what he had always wanted the mother of his children to feel, but thought it was impossible to find.

"How could any child born of love," he said softly, "be anything but good, brave and very, very beautiful?"

She looked up with shining eyes.

"You were happy when I loved you?" he asked.

"I did not . . know such . . happiness existed . . and we could still be on . . earth."

"That is what I felt," the Duke said, "and you are perfection itself."

"It is what I . . want you to think," Sarida whispered, "and . . please . . go on loving . . me."

"That is not only something I will do, but our love will grow and increase day by day and year by year. When we look back we will realise that while this is the beginning, there is so much more for us to discover."

Sarida made a little sound of happiness. Then she said:

"I . . I am a little afraid of . . going back to . . England. It is actually four years since I was last there and I was only fifteen."

As she spoke the Duke remembered that he had not yet told her who he really was.

Tomorrow, when they went aboard the *Sea Hawk* the crew would address him as 'Your Grace'.

Choosing his words carefully, he said:

"It may seem strange to you, my darling, but we have

133

been married without my having had time to explain to you so much you have to know about me."

She looked up at him in surprise.

He had the feeling she was a little nervous in case something was wrong.

"I came to Java at the request of Lord Curzon," the Duke explained quickly, "and I thought it would be a mistake to travel under my real name, because then the Dutch would have become too interested in me."

"Then . . your name is not . . Berry?" Sarida asked.

"Bury is my family name," he answered, "but I am in fact, the Duke of Inglebury!"

As he spoke he thought Sarida would be stunned into silence.

But to his surprise she exclaimed:

"Oh, I wish you had told Papa! He was so fond of your father!"

"Fond of my father?" the Duke asked in astonishment.

"They were friends, and I remember years ago when I was a child going with Papa to Ingle Castle."

For a moment the Duke was too surprised to say anything. Then he said:

"You have not told me the name of your house."

"It is Gale Priory," she answered, "and I suppose . . if you have been . . deceiving me . . I too have been deceiving you!"

"Gale Priory?" the Duke repeated. "Then your father was Lord Martyngale!"

"Like you," Sarida answered, "he had no wish to be fussed over by the Dutch or by the people of any other country we visited, so he used our family name of Martyn but spelt differently."

She laughed before she added:

"I never . . imagined you had anything to do with the Burys of Ingle castle because in my mind I spelt it B-E-R-R-Y."

134

"Lord Martyngale!" the Duke said beneath his breath.

He knew that Gale Priory, like his own house, was not only one of the most beautiful and outstanding houses in Buckinghamshire, but Lord Martyngale's ancestors went back in history like the Burys.

If anything, their lineage was even older than his.

Now what Sarida told him swept away any foreboding he had had about his family's likely reaction to his marriage.

In fact, he knew they would welcome her with open arms.

She could be everything they had hoped for in the Duchess of Inglebury.

He knew however that he would have married her whoever she was, even as he had thought, the daughter of some unknown author.

That she was not only spiritually and physically a part of him, but also materially made the story of their happiness even more wonderful than it was already.

He had no intention however, of letting Sarida know that he had worried in case the Burys looked down on her and thought she was the wrong wife for him.

He had been ready to protect her, even though it would be very difficult, from the sneers and criticism of other women.

Now that would not arise.

All he had to do was to ensure her happiness and preserve the spiritual link which had enabled them to find each other after so many centuries of being alone.

Sarida had been thinking over what he had said and now she whispered:

"I was right! I knew it was impossible for you to have behaved so badly since you were King Rakai Pikatan that you had to be reborn as somebody ordinary and unimportant."

The Duke gave a short laugh.

"I am not a King, my darling."

"I am sure an English Duke is nearly as important as a Hindu King from Java," Sarida smiled, "and he did not rule over the whole country!"

"I want to be important to you," the Duke said, "and I suppose, knowing how conceited the Gales are over their family tree you consider yourself superior to a Shailendra Princess!"

He was teasing her and Sarida put out her hand to pull his head down to hers.

"All I want to remember," she said, "is that I am grand enough to be your wife . . and that we are together . . just as we were sculpted together on the Temple, and will be together in England."

"You may be quite sure of that," the Duke said, "and, my darling, there are many things I can do at home to make myself more important than I am already, and because I will do them with you I shall lay them as tributes at your feet!"

"You are so wonderful . . so clever and so . . brave," Sarida said. "I am sure there is nothing you could not achieve if you set your heart on it."

"I have achieved you," the Duke said. "I have prevented you from worrying over our Temple, and I think, because the Sultan is aware of its importance, it will be safe until in more enlightened times all the Temples in Java will be restored to their original beauty."

"We must pray for that," Sarida said.

She spoke very seriously, but the Duke was aware of the softness of her body against his, and her lips ready to be kissed.

"That is all in the future," he said. "At the moment I am concerned with the present, and because you are so beautitful, and at the same time so ethereal, I am afraid you may disappear and I will find myself alone."

'How can you imagine that could happen?" Sarida asked. "If I disappear . . you will too, for we are one person! We may have already been through a hundred lives together, and perhaps spent some of them apart. Now this is the fulfilment that everyone seeks but only some are privileged to find."

"That is what I want to believe," the Duke said. "But we must be very careful, my precious, that in this world or the next we are never separated again!"

As if the idea frightened him he said violently:

"You are mine – mine completely, and I would kill anybody who tried to take you from me!"

Then he was kissing her, not softly or spiritually, but fiercely and demandingly.

"I am not a god!" he said. "I am a man and as a man I want you. Give me yourself as a woman – my woman – now and for ever!"

"I am . . yours . . completely yours," Sarida breathed. "Oh . . darling . . love me!"

Then there was only the light of the sun sinking in the sky and the soft breeze wafting over them like the Spirit of Java.

They were one with a love that came from eternity, went on to eternity, and for which there is no end.

OTHER BOOKS BY BARABARA CARTLAND

Romantic Novels, over 400, the most recently published being:

Secrets of the Heart
Riding to the Sky
Lovers in Lisbon
Love is Invincible
The Goddess of Love
An Adventure of Love
A Herb for Happiness
Only a Dream
Saved by Love
Little Tongues of Fire
A Chieftain Finds Love
The Lovely Liar
The Perfume of the Gods
A Knight in Paris
Revenge is Sweet
The Passionate Princess
Solita and the Spies
The Perfect Pearl
Love is a Maze
A Circus of Love
The Dream and the Glory (In aid of the St. John Ambulance Brigade)

Autiobiographical and biographical:
The Isthmus Years 1919-1939
The Years of Opportunity 1939-1945
I Search for Rainbows 1945-1976
We Danced All Night 1919-1929
Ronald Cartland (With a foreword by Sir Winston Churchill)
Polly – My Wonderful Mother
I seek the Miraculous

Historical:
Bewitching Women
The Outrageous Queen (The Story of Queen Christina of Sweden)
The Scandalous Life of King Carol
The Private Life of Charles II
The Private Life of Elizabeth, Empress of Austria
Josephine, Empress of France
Diane de Poitiers
Metternich – The Passionate Diplomat

Sociology:
You in the Home
The Fascinating Forties
Marriage for Moderns
Be Vivid, Be Vital
Love, Life and Sex
Vitamins for Vitality
Husbands and Wives
Men are Wonderful
Etiquette
The Many Facets of Love
Sex and the Teenager
The Book of Charm
Living Together
The Youth Secret
The Magic of Honey
The Book of Beauty and Health
Keep Young and Beautiful by Barbara Cartland and Elinor Glyn
Etiquette for Love and Romance
Barbara Cartland's Book of Health

Cookery:
Barbara Cartland's Health Food Cookery Book
Food for Love
Magic of Honey Cookbook
Recipes for Lovers
The Romance of Food

Editor of:
"The Common Problem" by Ronald Cartland (with a preface by the Rt. Hon. the Earl of Selborne, P.C.)
Barbara Cartland's Library of Love
Library of Ancient Wisdom
"Written with Love" Passionate love letters selected by Barbara Cartland

Drama:
Blood Money
French Dressing

Philosophy:
Touch the Stars

Radio Operetta:
The Rose and the Violet (Music by Mark Lubbock) Performed in 1942.

Radio Plays:
The Caged Bird: An episode in the life of Elizabeth Empress of Austria
Performed in 1957.

General:
Barbara Cartland's Book of Useless Information with a Foreword by the Earl Mountbatten of Burma.
(In aid of the United World Colleges)
Love and Lovers (Picture Book)
The Light of Love (Prayer Book)
Barbara Cartland's Scrapbook
(In aid of the Royal Photographic Museum)
Romantic Royal Marriages
Barbara Cartland's Book of Celebrities
Getting Older, Growing Younger

Verse:
Lines on Life and Love

Music:
An Album of Love Songs sung with the Royal Philharmonic Orchestra.

Films:
The Flame is Love
A Hazard of Hearts
Cartoons:
Barbara Cartland Romances (Book of Cartoons) has recently been published in the U.S.A., Great Britain, and other parts of the world.

Children:
A Children's Pop-Up Book: "Princess to the Rescue"

Barbara Cartland
A Circus of Love £1.95

Paralysed by fear, Thelma watched the ferocious tiger bound up the steps. The Earl tightened his arm around her . . .

Thelma knew her stepmother would stop at nothing to lay hands on a fortune. Only she would have thought of marrying her stepdaughter to her impecunious lover. The only safety lay in running away.

Journey's end came unexpectedly in a Big Top among lions, leopards and monkeys owned by the debonair but penniless Earl of Merstone.

Helping the Earl to save both his home and his menagerie without injuring his pride was one problem, foiling the wicked schemes of his cousin another – as was losing her heart. Together they made Thelma forget her own predicament until the day she so desperately needed a champion . . .

The Goddess of Love £1.95

Corena stepped off the gangway and ran to her father. As she flung her arms round him she pushed the revolver into his right hand . . .

While Corena waits for her father to return from Greece she receives a horrifying demand for ransom. Unless she delivers Lord Warburton, a noted collector of antiques shortly to visit Delphi, into the hands of bandits her father will be tortured to death!

Forbidden to tell Lord Warburton the truth, Corena is smuggled aboard his yacht. Discovery was inevitable – so was the mutual attraction that blossomed as sun-kissed days followed moonlit nights.

As they near their destination Corena's heart is torn asunder. How can she sacrifice the man she loves in order to save the father she adores . . .?

Barbara Cartland
Lovers in Lisbon £1.95

Are you sure my noble *Marques*, that you wish to mix your blue blood with the scrapings of the gutter?

Alone and starving, Felicita found it impossible to refuse the new life which the *Duchesse* de Monreuil offered. It was as if a fairytale had come true – especially when she met the irresistibly handsome *Marques* Alvare de Oliveira Vasconles.

How could Felicita have known she was to be the instrument of an all-consuming passion aimed like a vengeful sword at the heart and pride of one of Portugal's oldest families.

Strange and unexpected difficulties had to be overcome by Felicita and the *Marques* before Love proved more powerful than pride or poverty, greater than anything else in the whole world.

Sapphires in Siam £1.95

'You are the most infuriating girl I have ever met!' the Marquis exclaimed.

Refusing to believe her father had died in the Siamese jungle, Ankana was determined to accompany the Marquis of Vale on his voyage to Bangkok with or without his knowledge and approval.

The arrogant Marquis was used to dealing with riots, uprisings, hostile deserts and pirate infested seas. He was also used to having his own way. Unfortunately, none of these qualities were of great assistance in dealing with a lovely, unpredictable and impertinent young stowaway.

Though threatened by many dangers, Ankana persisted in the search which was to vindicate her innermost feelings and bring her the rapture of a love that would endure until the stars lost their glory and the seas ran dry.